WARNING:
DO NOT GIVE THIS BOOK TO YOUR OWN GRANDMA. SHE MIGHT GET IDEAS.

ORCHARD BOOKS

First published in Great Britain in 2018 by The Watts Publishing Group

1 3 5 7 9 10 8 6 4 2

Text copyright © Kita Mitchell 2018
Illustrations © Nathan Reed 2018

The moral rights of the author and illustrator have been asserted.

A CIP catalogue record for this book
is available from the British Library.

ISBN 978 1 40835 506 0

Printed and bound in Great Britain by
Clays Ltd, Elcograf S.p.A.

The paper and board used in this book are
made from wood from responsible sources.

Orchard Books
An imprint of Hachette Children's Group
Part of The Watts Publishing Group Limited
Carmelite House
50 Victoria Embankment
London EC4Y 0DZ

An Hachette UK Company
www.hachette.co.uk
www.hachettechildrens.co.uk

GRANDMA DANGEROUS AND THE DOG OF DESTINY

By Kita Mitchell

Illustrated by Nathan Reed

ORCHARD

For Beryl & Mitch

1

'What do you mean, you're not taking me?'

I could hardly believe what I was hearing. Was she serious?

'I'm sorry, Ollie.' Mum picked up her suitcase and plonked it on the sofa. 'It's not long till your exams. You can't have time off school before those. They're important.'

'Not as important as going to Clacton,' I said. 'There's a pier there, and an arcade. You have to take me. I love the seaside.'

I may as well not have spoken. Mum turned her back and walked into the kitchen. How rude! I could hear her pulling drawers open. 'Have you seen my sunglasses?' she called. 'I'm sure they were in here.'

I followed her. 'Two weeks won't matter,' I said.

'Two weeks in the whole scheme of things is nothing.' I looked at her, hopefully. 'It'd stop me worrying about Dad.'

Mum stopped rummaging. 'I'm sure Dad would prefer you to stay here studying,' she said.

'No, he wouldn't,' I said. 'Dad doesn't mind about stuff like that.'

'It's not like it's a holiday.'

'It sounds like one.'

'Well, it's not.' Mum popped some mosquito repellent in her bag. 'Poor Aunt Lucy – pecked in the eye by that parrot. SOMEONE has to go and look after her.'

'I didn't even know you had an Aunt Lucy. You've never mentioned her.'

Mum looked a bit flustered. 'Haven't I? She, um, came to stay at Christmas – years ago. Big hair and a fluffy cardi.'

I cast my mind back. Nope. It didn't ring a bell. Still, Mum had loads of aunts. I couldn't be expected to remember all of them.

'I told her safari parks were dangerous,' Mum said. 'Especially in nesting season. Let's hope she takes more notice of what I say in future.'

'You should have mentioned your award.' I said. 'You normally do.'

Mum looked proudly at the enormous trophy on the dresser. 'Don't be cheeky, Ollie. Being voted **Health and Safety Officer of the Year** was a huge honour. You have to admit – Great Potton is a much safer place these days.'

'Much more **boring**, you mean.'

Mum shook her head. 'Skateboards are lethal. So are rollerblades, conkers and chewing gum.

A complete ban was the only way.' She waved vaguely in my direction. 'Pass the sun cream, will you? That's right – the factor 150. You can't be too careful, even in March.'

I handed it to her. 'Please let me come,' I said. 'You can't leave me by myself, I'm only eleven. **It's against the law.**'

'I'm not leaving you by yourself,' Mum said. 'Of course I'm not.' She zipped up her bag. 'Grandma's coming to look after you. She's arriving in the morning.'

Grandma? I stared at Mum in horror. Oh no. Not Grandma Beatrix. I call her Grandma Boring. She's awful. She always goes on about manners, and checks me for nits.

'Unfortunately,' Mum went on, 'Grandma Beatrix is busy, so I had to ask Grandma Florence.'

My mouth fell open. **'Grandma Dangerous?'**

'Yes, Ollie. Grandma Dangerous.' Mum looked cross. 'Don't tell her I call her that, will you?'

'I won't,' I said.

I love Grandma Dangerous.

I was surprised, though. After last time, when there was an incident involving a trifle and a firework, Mum said she'd **NEVER** leave me alone with her again.

'Do you think you'll be all right?' Mum suddenly seemed a bit anxious. 'She's promised to be on her best behaviour.'

'Don't worry,' I said. 'I'm sure, after last time, she will be.'

Mum said she hoped so, and then she looked at me and I tried very hard to look mature and responsible and not to combust with joy.

Because, let's face it, Grandma's 'best behaviour' isn't very best at all.

2

Grandma Dangerous is **SO** much fun.

She's Dad's mum. He's an explorer and she is too. Well – she was until last year, anyway. She had to have a bit of time off after landing her hot-air balloon inside the rhino enclosure at Whipsnade Zoo.

'I could have sworn they were cows, Ollie,' she shouted over, as they wheeled her into the operating theatre.

Now she has a **false left leg**, and **very strong glasses**. Neither stop her getting into trouble – though, to be fair, the incident with the **firework** wasn't all her fault. And apart from the thing with the **rhinos**, everything usually turns out all right.

She makes Mum nervous. Mum's not a risk taker. She sees peril **everywhere**. That's why she's so good at her job. The most daring thing she does is knit.

'Watch the needles,' she'll shriek, if I walk past. **'They could have your eye out.'**

Mum wants me to be an accountant. She definitely doesn't want me to be an explorer. She won't even let me walk to school on my own. That's in case I get kidnapped. Mum thinks there are kidnappers on every corner, lying in wait to snatch me. And if I don't get kidnapped, then I might trip over a paving stone and get concussion, or someone's garden wall might choose the very second I walk past to topple and if Mum wasn't there to save me then where would I be? Kidnapped or concussed or squashed, obviously.

When someone spends all their time making sure that nothing bad happens to you, it is **VERY ANNOYING.**

I wish she'd stop worrying. I think it's because I'm an only child. She used to talk about having another baby, but in the end, we just got a hamster.

Dad doesn't worry about anything. He tries to make out that Mum married him because 'opposites

11

attract', but I know that wasn't the reason. They just met at a party where the music was loud.

Mum: *Lovely to meet you, Henry. What do you do?*

Dad: *I'm an explorer. Just back from the rainforest.*

Mum: *An insurer? Just back from the main office? That's wonderful. Shall we dance?*

Mum only realised her mistake on their honeymoon, as they were about to go over **Niagara Falls** in a barrel.

To be fair, she was right to worry when Dad announced that he was going to fly around the world in a plane he'd built himself. He insisted he'd be perfectly safe, but the last time we heard from him he'd just crashed into a swamp. He said he was 'absolutely fine' and was calling from the top of a large tree, which he'd climbed to escape an angry crocodile.

He was just about to tell us which country he was

in, when his mobile cut out. We tried to ring him back, but he didn't answer.

I guess there aren't many places to charge your phone in a swamp.

I'm sure he's all right. He'll be surviving on berries and nuts and slowly making his way back to civilisation.

He has absolutely,

definitely

not been eaten.

Sometimes, though, when I lie awake at night and think about it, I'm not so certain. Three weeks is an awfully long time to be lost, especially in a reptile-infested swamp.

3

The next day I was woken up by Mum banging about downstairs, and then she started hoovering, which I thought was a bit inconsiderate on a Sunday before nine o'clock. She always tidies loads before we have visitors – though I'd have thought that as it was Grandma who was coming, there was no need to bother.

Personally, I didn't feel like doing any unnecessary cleaning, so I spent ages getting dressed and by the time I got downstairs Mum had put the hoover away and was sticking instructions on everything. I read a few. Mum was worried as usual. Worried that Grandma would forget to feed me, or let me watch too much telly, or send me to school with crisps instead of fruit.

She kept trying to hug me. 'You'll be fine,' she said. 'There's loads of food and the emergency money's in the tin in the cupboard. Don't let Grandma spend it on cigars, will you?'

'She said she'd given up,' I said.

'And make sure she gets you to school by eight forty-five. I've reminded her again and again about your exams coming up.'

'Yes, Mum.'

'Your homework timetable is on the kitchen door, and, just in case, there's another copy on the fridge. Maths on Monday, English on Tuesday, Maths again on Wednes—'

'Yes, Mum. I know.'

'She'll be here any minute. What have I forgotten?' She looked around frantically. *'The shower. I haven't left instructions on the shower.'* She raced upstairs.

'Mum,' I shouted after her. 'Grandma's nearly sixty. I expect she knows how to use a shower.'

'Not necessarily,' Mum said. 'She's spent most of her life in a tent. Do you think I need to label the toilet paper?'

I decided not to get involved with any more

labelling decisions and went to the door to wait. I was sure I could hear a car. Grandma's got an old Mini. Mum and Dad bought it for her after her balloon was wrecked by the rhinos. She wasn't very grateful. She said it was boring. I helped her paint it. It's definitely not boring now.

There she was! Yay!

The Mini hurtled into the driveway, ploughed through Mum's flower bed and slammed into the hedge. Grandma says she's passed her test, but sometimes I wonder.

'Ollie!' She wound down the window and stuck

her head out. 'Great to see you! Isn't this just **amazeballs?'**

'Hi, Grandma,' I said. 'Do you need any help?'

'I'm fine.' She forced open the door and scrambled out through the foliage. 'I'll tell you, Ollie, I could hardly believe it when I got that call from your mum – never in a MILLION TRILLION Sundays did I think I'd be asked to keep an eye on you again – and for two whole weeks!'

I ran over to give her a hug but she suddenly ducked down behind a spotted laurel. 'What are you doing?' I asked.

'Get down!' she hissed. 'There's a car coming.'

'So?'

'What colour is it?'

I peered down the street. 'Blue.'

Grandma winced. 'Drat. Can you see who's driving? It's not two awful-looking men is it? One bald? One wearing a disgusting mustard-coloured scarf?'

'It's Beryl,' I said. 'From number seventy-seven.'

'Phew.' Grandma got to her feet and brushed off a bit of mud. 'Thank goodness for that. Let's get inside.'

She was up to something. There wasn't much point asking what, though. **Grandma always denies everything.**

'How do I look?' she asked, as we walked towards the house. 'I made quite an effort – I didn't want your mum to change her mind and not go.'

Grandma usually wears clothes crocheted from the beards of Icelandic monks (so she says). Today though, she was dressed in a long tweed skirt and a matching jacket. She'd even brushed her hair. 'You look nice,' I said, politely.

'But will she approve, Ollie? She's very hard to please. Do you remember her fancy-dress party? When I came as the Emperor in his new clothes? I never heard such a fuss.'

'That was more to do with what you *weren't* wearing, Grandma.' I pushed open the door. 'Mum? Where are you?'

'Hello, Florence.' Mum appeared on the landing. 'I'm just ... Oh. You look smart.'

'Respectable,' Grandma said. 'Respectable, responsible and MORE than capable of looking after my grandson for two weeks, **unsupervised**.' She gave me a nudge.

'Well, yes. Let's see about that, shall we?' Mum didn't look particularly convinced, but she came downstairs and gave Grandma a kiss on the cheek. 'Now, I'll have to go soon, so come into the kitchen and let me show you—'

'The homework and revision schedule? Is this it, here on the fridge?' Grandma rushed over. 'Wonderful. A small boy can **NEVER** have enough homework and revision. These days, exams count for so much. I mean – imagine if he should fail them? Poor Ollie – on the scrapheap at eleven.' Grandma was being a bit too enthusiastic. I gave a little cough to remind her not to overdo it.

Mum frowned. 'I'm sure it won't come to that. He's very bright. If he wanted, he could be an accountant. Now, I was going to show you where to put your luggage, but I can run through the schedule if you'd prefer?'

'I'd like nothing better,' Grandma said. 'Ollie, dear. My bags are in the car. Would you bring them in?'

'OK,' I said. 'All of them?'

'Yes. All of them.' She handed me the keys and checked to make sure Mum was out of earshot. 'Be careful with the biggest one,' she whispered. 'Take that one straight upstairs. Don't drop it – **and whatever you do, don't look inside.'**

4

Grandma shouldn't have said that, because as soon as she did, I wanted to know what was in the bag more than anything! She *must* have brought me a present.

I dashed back outside and opened the car boot. A few things toppled out on to the ground. Nothing exciting. Sandwich wrappers, apple cores, half an old cake. You'd have thought that someone Grandma's age would use a bin, but obviously not. I pulled out a carrier bag full of socks and moved her coat (the one she says she hand-stitched from **yeti skin** but which has a label saying '*Made in Basingstoke*').

There it was. I could see it. A tartan holdall underneath a telescope and a camping stove.

I reached in and grabbed the straps. It wasn't heavy. I'd almost got it all the way out, when it **wiggled**

I was so surprised, I dropped it. **Eh? Had it wiggled?** I was sure it had wiggled. Not the bag. The bag hadn't wiggled. Something inside the bag had wiggled. <u>SOMETHING ALIVE</u>.

I peered down at it. Grandma had expressly said not to drop it. Never mind. It had landed on the yeti coat.

I stared at it. What could it be? I wanted to know. I wanted to know really badly, but I didn't dare open it. I didn't want to get Grandma into trouble. I was going to have to wait till Mum had gone.

I carried the bag into the house and up to the spare room. It didn't move again. Maybe whatever was in there had gone to sleep? I hoped it wasn't a snake, or anything dangerous. Something cute would be nice. A chipmunk, maybe – or a pot-bellied mini-pig?

I brought the rest of Grandma's stuff up. The bag sat quietly where I'd left it by the bed. I gave it a prod. Had I imagined it? Perhaps there wasn't anything inside, after all.

I decided it'd be OK to open the zip a teeny bit, to check. If nothing slithered out, I could open it a bit more and have a proper look. If I needed to, I could do it up again, really quickly.

I was just reaching out when Mum shouted from downstairs.

'OLLIE?'

Bum.

'WHERE ARE YOU, OLLIE? I'VE GOT TO GO SOON.'

I stood up and gave the bag one last look. It'd have to wait.

Back in the kitchen, Mum was giving Grandma some final instructions. Grandma was nodding furiously. 'Yes, Sukey, kidnappers on every corner ... you're right, not like the good old days of running

23

free ... absolutely **NOTHING** out of packets ... Oh, Ollie. There you are at last. Your mother and I have been going through her lists. **I completely agree with everything on them.'**

'Oh?' I said.

Grandma was looking very earnest. She almost looked like she meant every word she said. I hoped Mum hadn't brainwashed her while I was bringing the bags in.

'This is a crucial time in your life, young man. Your exams come first. And that means healthy eating, early to bed, and lots of studying.'

This wasn't sounding good.

'Furthermore,' said Grandma, 'I have promised your mother that, while she is away, I'll do my absolute best not to get you into any, ahem, "pickles" – life-threatening or otherwise.'

I thought about the bag upstairs.

It probably was a snake.

Grandma's such a good liar.

'Don't worry,' I said. 'I'll be fine.'

Mum's taxi arrived then, so there wasn't a chance to run through my revision schedule one more time, which was a shame. I did get a hug though. It went on for ages and almost suffocated me and then Mum looked like she was going to cry.

'Gracious,' Grandma said. 'Pull yourself together, Sukey. It's only two weeks and Clacton is practically down the road. Get a move on – that taxi's on a meter.'

I picked up Mum's suitcase as she put on her coat.

'Come on, come on.' Grandma ushered Mum out. 'You don't want to miss your plane.'

'Train,' said Mum. **'Not plane**, Florence. I'm going to Clacton, remember. By **train.'**

'Of course you are. Clacton. By **train**. That's right. Ha ha. My mistake. Have you got everything? Ticket? Credit card? Loo roll in case you're caught short?'

'Yes,' said Mum, as Grandma shoved her into the back seat. 'I'm very organised.'

'Off you go, then,' said Grandma. 'Have a safe trip.

25

Give my regards to Aunt Lucy.'

That was weird. Grandma just winked at Mum. *Why would she wink?*

'Bye, Mum,' I said.

Mum wound down the window. 'Bye, Ollie. Bye, Florence.' Her voice shook a bit and she reached into her bag for a tissue. 'I'll call you in a couple of days.'

I leant in and gave her a kiss. I wouldn't normally as I'm far too old for that sort of thing, especially in public – but she did look upset and no one was watching apart from Grandma. 'You will let me know if you hear from Dad, won't you?' I said.

'Of course,' she said. 'I'll see you soon, sweetheart.'

The driver started the engine and I stepped back out of the way. Mum gave one last wave, and Grandma and I watched until the taxi turned the corner at the end of the street.

5

Back in the kitchen, Grandma flopped on to a chair and announced she needed a cup of tea. Apparently, all the '*agreeing with Mum*' had been very tiring and we couldn't possibly start having fun until she was revived. She ordered me to put the kettle on, which I thought was a bit rich considering she was supposed to be looking after **me**! I couldn't be bothered to argue, though. I had other things on my mind.

'Grandma,' I said. 'Why did you wink at Mum?'

Grandma looked puzzled. 'Wink?' she said. 'I didn't wink, Ollie. There was definitely no winking when your mum left for Aus— I mean, **Clacton**. Now, hurry up! I'm parched over here.'

I filled the kettle and switched it on.

'That bag,' I said. 'What's in it?'

She completely ignored me! She just stood up and

asked where Mum kept the biscuits. 'There's no point in a cup of tea without them,' she said.

'There aren't any. Grandma, wha—'

'You'll have to go and get some. Here – use the money from this tin.'

'That's for emergencies,' I said.

'Ollie, there is no greater emergency than no biscuits. There you go – thirty pounds. That should keep us in custard creams for a couple of days.'

Thirty pounds? On biscuits?

'No need to hurry back.'

Before I could open my mouth to argue, she'd marched me down the hallway and out the front door. She slammed it behind me. How rude! She was definitely up to something. I bent down to peer through the letterbox, but the door swung open again.

'What are you doing, Ollie? I just wanted to remind you not to talk to any strange men, especially **bald ones**, or ones with **mustard-coloured scarves.**'

'Oh.' I blinked. 'OK.'

'And one other thing – while you're there, could you pick me up a tin of dog food?'

'Dog food?' I said. 'What for?'

'For the hedgehogs.'

'Eh?'

'I saw some in the garden earlier. Darling little things. They adore dog food. In fact, get two tins. Two tins should be plenty.' She slammed the door again.

Hedgehogs? I didn't know we had hedgehogs. I love hedgehogs!

When I got to the shop, **PIPER** was sitting on the wall outside, chewing on her pigtail. She's in my year at school, and has so many freckles her face is almost orange.

I don't like her. She's annoying. She always says exactly what she thinks. Last week, when we were in the lunch queue, she asked if they'd 'found any of my dad' yet!

She looked surprised to see me, and her pigtail dropped out of her mouth. 'Out on your own?' she asked.

'I think you'll find,' I said, 'most eleven-year-olds are allowed out "on their own".'

She jumped down and followed me into the shop. **'You're not,'** she said. 'In case you get **kidnapped**. Where's your mum? Has she been arrested for making things too safe?'

I ignored her and took a basket from the stack.

'What are you getting?'

I thought about ignoring her again, but I knew she'd just keep on. 'Dog food,' I said. 'And biscuits.' I picked up some Hobnobs. 'Thirty pounds worth of biscuits, actually.'

'Blimey! That's a lot.' She looked impressed.

I scowled at her, but she didn't go away.

'Sorry for what I said about your dad,' she said. 'It came out wrong. Any chance of a Jaffa Cake?'

'Nope,' I said. 'Won't your mum be wondering

where you are?'

'Probably not.' She followed me to the pet food aisle. 'I didn't know you had a dog,' she said. 'I thought you weren't allowed one. You know – because of all the diseases in their poop?'

'It's for the hedgehogs, actually,' I said.

Piper giggled. 'If you did have a dog,' she said, 'it could protect you from all those kidnappers your mum goes on about.'

Sometimes I can't believe Piper's the same age as me. **She's so childish**. I turned my back on her and started looking at the tins. Dog food was really expensive! I hoped I wouldn't have to put any of the biscuits back.

'Ollie?'

'What?' I said.

'Those blokes next to the Woofy-Chunks look a bit dodgy.'

'You sound like my mum,' I said.

She poked my arm. 'Seriously,' she said.

'They're coming over.'

I looked up the aisle. Oh. There were two men pushing an empty trolley and heading straight for us. One was short and **bald** and a bit sweaty. The other had a **ponytail** and a **mustard-coloured scarf** wrapped around his face.

I stepped forward to get out of their way but they didn't walk past. They stopped. **The back of my neck prickled**. Maybe Mum had been right about kidnappers all along!

The man with the scarf picked up a box of doggy chews and dropped it into his trolley. Then he stepped sideways on to my foot, which hurt.

'Sorry,' he said. He didn't look sorry.

I started edging away, but it was too late. Piper never missed an opportunity to chat. 'Why are you wearing your scarf like that?' she said. 'Aren't you hot?'

The man tapped the side of his nose. 'We're investigating a theft.' He looked around shiftily.

'I'M IN DISGUISE.'

'Oh,' said Piper 'Why do you nee—'

I gave her a nudge. 'You're not supposed to talk to strangers,' I said.

Piper shrugged. 'Just making conversation,' she said.

'I think we should go.'

'What about the dog food?' She picked up a tin of Small Dog's Delight. 'You should get this one. If you find a golden bone on the inside of the lid you get **twenty thousand pounds!**'

'They're a con,' I said. 'No one ever wins.'

'Actually,' said the man with the scarf, 'we won an egg cup from the back of a cereal packet once. It was a really nice egg cup. Mum made us take turns wi—'

'**SHUT UP, ED,**' said Bert. 'Remember why we're here.'

'Oh yes,' said Ed. He tugged his scarf down a bit and pointed at the tin in Piper's hands. 'Dog food, eh?' he said. 'That means you must be the owner of a lovely little doggy?'

'It's for the hedgehogs, actually,' she said. 'Ollie's mum would never let him have a dog. You know, in case it savaged him, or gave him fleas.'

I scowled at her. 'I could have one if I wanted,' I said.

Bert sighed. 'We used to have one,' he said. 'Until this morning, that is, when he was stolen. That's why we're here. Watching for anyone suspicious buying dog food.'

'What sort of dog was it?' asked Piper.

'Let me show you.' Bert reached inside his jacket and pulled out a photo. 'There you go.'

Piper squinted at it. 'Are you sure it's a dog?' she said. 'He's ever so small.'

I peered over her shoulder. It was a dog. A very tiny, scruffy one. His frizzy grey coat stuck out from everywhere – apart from his legs, which were bald.

'He's rare,' Bert said. **'VERY** rare. An Egyptian Choodle. **WORTH A FORTUNE.'** He leant closer and dropped his voice. 'Perhaps you two could keep an eye out? Let us know if you see him?'

'Sure.' Piper took the picture. 'I guess there's a reward, seeing as he's so valuable?'

'Of course. My number's on the back. Call if you see anything. Anything at all.'

6

I paid for the biscuits and the tins of Small Dog's Delight, and we had three pounds left over. Piper said we should go to the park and spend it on ice cream, but I wanted to get home and see what Grandma was up to.

'Shouldn't you be going?' I said to Piper. 'I expect your mum's worried about you.'

'Oh, no.' Piper jogged to keep up. 'My mum's not like yours. There's so many of us she never knows where any of us are – apart from the twins, because they can't get out of their cots yet. It must be awful being an only child. Bet you can't get away with anything.'

'Maybe,' I said. 'But at least I don't have to share any of my stuff.'

Piper shrugged. 'I don't have any stuff to share,' she said.

I felt a bit sorry for her. I even started to think about letting her have a biscuit. Nothing with chocolate on, but maybe a custard crea—

'Ollie?'

'What?' I said.

'Can you smell smoke?'

I sniffed the air. 'Where's it coming from?'

'Don't know,' said Piper, as we walked around the corner. 'But there's a fire engine outside your house.'

GRANDMA!

I started to run. Mum would go crazy if Grandma burnt the house down. I charged through the gate and up the path. The door was open so I stopped to check for flames (I came top in *Fire Safety* at Scouts) but I couldn't see any.

'HELLO?' I shouted. **'HELLO?'**

'The fire must be out.' Piper pushed past me. 'Come on.'

The hallway was soaking. 'I guess your mum's away?' said Piper as we sloshed up it. 'Yup.' I pushed open the kitchen door. 'She is.'

BLIMEY. There was a whole load of firemen. Most were chatting and drinking tea, though one had a broom and was sweeping up some ash. Grandma was over by the sink. She looked OK. Not singed, or anything.

'Ollie!' She waved the kettle at me. 'There you are. Have you got the biscuits?'

I handed her the bag. 'I thought Mum told you not to do any cooking?' I said.

'Silly – you know I don't cook.' Grandma took out some Jaffa Cakes. 'Who's your friend?'

'She's not my friend, actually,' I said.

Piper stuck her hand out. 'Hello, Ollie's gran,' she said. 'I'm Piper.'

'Lovely name,' said Grandma. 'Biscuit?'

Piper took the packet. 'Shall I hand them round?'

Honestly! Piper was never this polite at school. **What a suck-up!**

Grandma patted me on the shoulder. 'I expect

you're wondering what happened, Ollie?'

'It wasn't your gran's fault,' said one of the firemen. He helped himself to a Jaffa Cake.

'Thanks, Bill,' said Grandma. 'Take two.'

'What wasn't your fault?' I said.

Grandma shook her head. 'It's awful,' she said. 'You'll probably never forgive me.'

'It's not Myrtle, is it?' I looked at her cage in a panic. Maybe she'd been overcome by fumes?

'Your hamster's fine, Ollie. It's worse than that. Much worse.'

Eh? What could be worse than something happening to Myrtle?

Grandma dabbed her eye. 'I can hardly find the words.'

'Don't be too hard on her,' said Bill. He took another Jaffa Cake.

Grandma took a deep breath. She closed her eyes. 'I'm so sorry. It's your mum's lists.'

'Mum's lists?'

'Yes.' Grandma nodded mournfully. *'They're gone.* All those schedules and instructions that she spent so long over. I'd gathered them together on the table – I mean, I was **desperate** to learn how to work the vacuum, and discover which night was **maths night** – and, oh, Ollie, you'll never guess ...'

'What?'

'They caught fire.'

'Caught fire?'

'Yes,' said Grandma. 'Just like that! I wasn't having a cigar, Ollie, I promise you. I merely struck a match – and accidentally dropped it. Never play with matches, children. The whole lot went up. **Pouf**. And then that nosy old bag next door saw the smoke and called the fire brigade.'

'So you burnt all the lists – by accident?'
I looked at her suspiciously.

'I didn't do it on purpose.' Grandma popped a whole Jaffa Cake into her mouth. 'I'd **never** do that.'

It took ages to get rid of all the firemen. That was Mum's fault. If she hadn't made Great Potton so safe they'd have better things to do than sit around and eat biscuits.

As soon as they'd left, I started to think about the bag upstairs, but I didn't want to ask in front of Piper. She still hadn't gone home. She'd made herself a mug of tea and was watching *Cake Off* on the telly.

'What a sweetheart,' said Grandma. 'Is she your girlfriend?'

I almost choked on the last Hobnob. **'NO,'** I said, as coldly as I could. **'SHE IS NOT.'** I couldn't imagine anything worse. I mean, if I had a girlfriend it wouldn't be someone who came around uninvited and scarfed all the Wagon Wheels. It would be someone with MANNERS and shiny blonde hair –

like Thea Harris, who sits on my table in maths and lets me borrow her protractor.

'I've asked her to stay for supper,' said Grandma, brushing ash off the table. 'What is there?'

'I don't know,' I said. 'Mum left you in charge of food and stuff.' I looked across the hallway into the living room. Piper had her feet up on the coffee table. She was going to be here all night! I couldn't wait any longer. I wouldn't wait any longer. I took a deep breath and faced Grandma.

'What's wrong, dear?' asked Grandma. 'Have you got a tummy ache? That's your mum's fault – you're not used to eating biscuits.'

'I want to know what's upstairs.' I said.

'Three bedrooms and a bathroom, I think,' said Grandma.

'You know what I'm talking about,' I said. **'What's in that tartan bag?'**

Grandma stuck her head into the fridge. 'How about veggie burgers?' she said. 'I'm sure they're very nutritious.'

Right. I'd given Grandma enough chances to tell me.

I was going to go and look.

I bounded upstairs. The tartan holdall was still by the bed. I hesitated.

Suppose it was something dangerous?

I mean, Grandma had told me not to look inside.

What if it was a snake??

'Ollie?' Piper called from downstairs. 'Where are you? It's the Celebration Sponge Finale!'

I knew what Piper was like. If I didn't reply she'd be up here in a minute. I grabbed the bag and tugged at the zip. Then I jumped back and waited, holding my breath.

Nothing moved.

 Nothing slid out.

That was odd.

I leant forward and peered inside. Eh? The bag was empty!

I mean, it wasn't completely empty. There were some massive pants in there, and a bra. **GROSS**. I pulled them out to look underneath. Nothing. Nothing at all. Not even a tree frog.

Whatever was in the bag had gone. *Grandma must have hidden it.*

'Ollie?'

I could hear footsteps on the stairs. Two pairs. I started stuffing everything back.

I wasn't quick enough.

'Ollie?' said Grandma. 'What are you doing with my smalls?'

'They're not very small,' I said.

'No need to be rude,' Grandma huffed.

Piper giggled. 'I thought they were yours, Ollie,' she said.

I ignored her and looked at Grandma. 'What have you done with it?' I asked.

'Done with what?'

'There was something in here. *I didn't imagine it.*'

'Something in where?' said Piper.

'Grandma?'

Grandma scowled. 'Oh, all right,' she said. 'I was going to tell you. I was waiting for the right moment.'

'Tell me what?' I said.

'I **didn't steal** him.'

'Steal what?' Piper looked confused.

'I *found* him.' Grandma headed for the door. 'Come on. I'll show you.'

We followed her across the landing to Mum's room. 'There you go.' She gave me a little push. 'Take a look.'

The bump under Mum's flowery duvet was guinea pig-sized. That didn't mean it was a guinea pig. It could well be a flesh-eating vampire bat. I approached cautiously.

'Get on with it,' said Piper.

Honestly! It was all right for her, standing behind me!

I took a deep breath. Right. I pulled off the duvet really quickly and then took a step back.

Eh?

It wasn't a flesh-eating vampire bat.

It was a dog.

It wasn't any old dog, though.

It looked exactly like Bert and Ed's dog.

It couldn't be Bert and Ed's dog. Why would Grandma have Bert and Ed's dog?

'Oh, wow!' Piper shoved me out of the way. 'Look at him! *He's tiny*! **He's adorable**! Look at his fur, Ollie. He's got an afro. Can I wake him up?'

The dog half-opened one eye and glared at her.

'I think you just did,' I said.

'What do you think, Ollie?' Grandma clasped her hands. 'He's a charmer, isn't he?'

My eyes watered. 'Could someone open a window?' I said. **'He really smells.'**

'You have such a sensitive nose, Ollie.' Piper scooped the dog up and held him in the air. 'He's gorgeous! Look at his lovely grey curls.'

Grandma looked proud. 'Would you like a hold, Ollie?'

'Thanks, but no,' I said. 'And keep him away from Myrtle.'

Piper rumpled the dog's coat. 'It looks like an Egyptian Choodle,' she said. 'But it can't be. They're very rare. Where did you get him, Ollie's gran?'

Grandma gazed nonchalantly out of the window. 'Didn't I say? I thought I had.'

'No, you didn't,' I said. I was starting to feel a tiny bit suspicious.

'I'm sure I did,' Grandma said. 'Well, dear. I was driving along, on the way here, this morning, and there he was, just sitting by the side of the road. Tragic, it was, tragic. **He'd obviously been abandoned.** I pulled over and opened the door, and in he hopped.'

'So if you found him, why did you hide him?' I asked.

'Well, you know, Ollie – your mother! I couldn't risk her finding out I had an animal with me. I thought it best to wait till she was safely on her way. I didn't want the neighbours sending a text and grassing me up. She'd have been back in two shakes of a duck's bum, wagging her finger and tutting.'

'I can't believe you let a dog sleep in her bed,' I said. 'I won't mention that when she calls.'

'Probably best,' said Grandma. 'She'd go absolutely bananas. Anyway. There he was, just sitting there. *I certainly didn't take him from two men at a service station.* Because that would be stealing – and as I always say, Ollie, stealing is very wrong.'

Piper and I looked each other. Then we looked at Grandma.

'You stole Bert and Ed's dog, didn't you?' I said.

'You really stole their dog,' said Piper in delight. 'That's so bad.'

Grandma looked indignant. 'I did not **steal** him,' she huffed. 'I **rescued** him. I admit the circumstances

49

may be a teensy bit different from my original explanation – but when you hear what I have to say, I think you will agree that I absolutely did the right thing.'

8

Grandma sat down on the bed. She took a tissue from the box on the bedside table and dabbed at the corner of her eye.

'There's no need to fake cry,' I said.

Grandma looked huffy. 'On this occasion, Ollie,' she said, 'these are genuine tears of distress. Heartless, some people are, the way they treat their animals.'

'He doesn't look badly treated,' I said. 'Just scruffy.'

'Do you want to hear this or not? Anyway, there I was, this morning, stopping off for a wee at the service station – you know me, Ollie, when I need to go, I need to go. Remember that time at the stately home? I don't know why they made such a fuss. It's what chamber pots are for.'

How could I forget? Mum had trouble renewing her National Trust membership after that.

'Anyway, I'd come out of the ladies, and got into the queue to buy some cigars – ahem, I mean **Polos** – when I saw two horrible men dragging this poor little doggy behind them.'

'Bert and Ed?' said Piper.

'Well, they didn't introduce themselves, but I suppose so,' said Grandma. 'They pushed in front of me, and asked for fifty scratch cards—'

'Fifty?' I said.

'Yes. Fifty.'

'Blimey,' said Piper. 'Why would you buy that many, all at once?'

'They must have felt lucky,' said Grandma. 'I've no idea why. **No idea at all**. Well. They went and sat down and were scratching away, and – not that I was listening or anything, because you know me, Ollie, I would 𝕟𝕖𝕧𝕖𝕣 eavesdrop – but I overheard the bald one say that if the dog didn't get his act together soon, they'd sell him to McDoodoos for burger meat!'

'Well, that's not very nice,' Piper said. 'Poor little doggy.'

'What did they mean, get his act together?' I asked. 'Does he do tricks?'

Grandma ignored me. 'I was about to tell them not to be so mean, when they said something about nipping to the loo. I seized the opportunity. I kindly offered to pet-sit while they went to the gents' – and as soon as they turned the corner, I legged it.'

'That's **proper** stealing,' said Piper, in admiration. 'Well done.'

'Thanks,' said Grandma. 'Anyway, I dashed to my car and hid the little sweetie in the boot. I was out of there before those thugs had even flushed.'

'Wow,' said Piper. 'You're amazing.'

'I can't believe you stole a dog,' I said.

'I can hardly believe it myself,' said Grandma, proudly. 'I drove like the wind. All the way here.'

I remembered Grandma ducking down behind the spotted laurel. I looked at her accusingly. 'They followed you, didn't they?' I said. 'That's why they were in the shop.'

'Absolutely not, Ollie,' Grandma said. 'I mean, they might have chased me for a while, but once I'd gone three times around the Tesco roundabout and across the village green, they were nowhere to be seen.'

'What's his name?' Piper asked. She lifted the little tag on his collar. **'Anubis the Ninth,'** she said. 'Anubis? Poor thing. What a dreadful name. Imagine being landed with that.'

'It's the name of an Egyptian god, actually,' I said. 'The god of lost things. And he is an Egyptian Choodle, so it's not that silly.'

'Whatever,' Piper said. 'I wonder how much he's worth.'

'He's priceless to me.' Grandma snatched the dog back. 'I can't imagine life without him.'

'He smells,' I said.

'I'll give him a bath,' Piper said. 'He'd like that.'

'What an excellent idea,' said Grandma.

'Where are the guest towels?'

I wasn't sure we should handle stolen goods, but Piper had already rushed into the bathroom and turned on the taps. I didn't see why she should have all the fun. I went to find Mum's nice shampoo.

It turned out Anubis didn't want a bath. As soon as I lifted him in, he yapped and yapped and tried to bite me with his tiny little teeth. In the end I had to hold him down with an exfoliating mitt.

'Have you got any conditioner?' Piper asked.

'On the shelf,' I said, wiping soap out of my eye.

Piper rummaged through the bottles. 'Hey, Ollie. Look!' She held up a box. 'Hair dye. Butterscotch Blonde. That should cover the grey.'

'I don't expect he cares about being grey,' I said. 'He's a dog, not my mum.'

Piper looked at me. 'It's in case we bump into Bert and Ed,' she said. 'They won't recognise him.'

Oh. Right.

Anubis liked the dye even less than the shampoo.

There was a lot of struggling. I ended up doing the hard work, of course. Piper stood at a safe distance and hosed him down.

'The colour suits him,' she said. 'But he's still small and frizzy and Choodle-like.'

'He won't be in a minute.' Grandma stuck her head around the door. 'I've found some hair straighteners. Come along, Piper. Bring Anubis. Ollie? You look a bit wet. You'd better get changed.'

In the time it took for me to put on dry clothes and mop the floor a bit, Anubis had been transformed. 'Was he supposed to turn out like that?' I said. 'He looks like a long-haired guinea pig.'

'That's the point,' Piper said. **'HE'S IN DISGUISE.'**

They'd done a good job. He didn't look the same at all. There wasn't a curl left on him. His coat was smooth and glossy and trailed along the floor. Some of it had been combed into bunches and tied with bright pink ribbon. They sprouted gaily from behind his ears.

Grandma had propped
a mirror against the
skirting board, and
every now and then Anubis
strutted up and down in
front of it, as if he was
admiring himself.

'What's with the bows?' I asked.

'We're going to call him Rose,' Grandma said. 'Just for the time being.'

'Rose?' I said. 'Isn't he a boy?'

'Yes, Ollie. It's part of the cover.'

'But he's got a – you know – *a thingy*,' I said.

'Well, no one's going to look, are they?' Grandma tutted. 'Who would be so rude?'

I was pleased there was no sign of Piper when I came down for breakfast. She'd stayed so late trying to teach Rose tricks, I wasn't sure if she'd even gone home.

Grandma was up, and Rose was standing on the table scoffing Small Dog's Delight out of a teacup. Bits were flying everywhere. It smelt disgusting. I wondered if Grandma had remembered to check the tin for a golden bone. I was about to ask her when I spotted the Twinkle Flakes.

'Are those for breakfast?'

'I'm afraid so, Ollie. Your mum's home-made muesli **accidentally** fell in the bin.'

'That's a shame,' I said.

'Isn't it? I had to nip to the shop. I was going to buy something healthy, but they'd ... um ... sold out. I got these and Marshmallow Fudge Waffles instead. I hope that's ok?'

'I guess it'll have to do,' I said, reaching for the Twinkle Flakes and pouring myself a massive bowlful. Rose finished slurping his mush and trotted over to see what I'd got. I put my arm in the way. I wasn't sharing – **not after ten years of high fibre.**

'Why are you wearing your school uniform?' Grandma asked.

'It's Monday,' I said. 'Isn't it?'

'Silly,' said Grandma. 'I've phoned in sick for you. Could you pass the sugar?'

'You don't actually need sugar on Twinkle Flakes, Grandma. What do you mean, "phoned in sick"?'

'You can never have too much sugar.' Grandma tipped some into her bowl. 'You've got scarlet fever. A raging temperature, a swollen tongue and a purple rash. Nil by mouth. You're terribly weak. **In fact, you might die.** They're not expecting you back for a month – if at all. Waffle?'

'If at all?' I blinked. **'What about my exams?'**

Grandma sighed loudly. 'It's a terrible shame,' she said, 'but you're going to have to miss them.'

Well, I didn't mind – but Mum might. 'I think they're important,' I said.

'I'm sure they are.' Grandma fed Rose a bit of waffle. 'But not as important as finding your dad.'

Eh? I put down my spoon. 'Sorry?' I said. 'What did you say?'

'Isn't Rose a sweetheart? Such dainty manners.' She fed him another bit. 'What did I say about what?'

'FINDING DAD?'

'Dad? Oh, yes. That's right.' Grandma leant down and picked up her handbag. She started to rifle through it. 'I promised Sukey I wouldn't say anything – but I've changed my mind. I don't see why she should have all the fun.'

Now I was really confused. 'You mean the pier?' I said.

'No. Not the pier. **AUSTRALIA**.'

'Australia?'

'Keep up, Ollie. **Your mum's gone to Australia**.'

I stared at her. 'No, she hasn't. She's gone to Clacton.'

'That's what she told you.' Grandma pulled a crumpled sheet of paper out of her bag and started smoothing it out.

'But she went to look after Aunt Lucy.'

Grandma looked at me mournfully. 'I'm so sorry, Ollie. **There is no Aunt Lucy**.'

I looked at her in horror. 'Did she die?'

'She doesn't exist.'

'She does,' I said. 'She's got big hair and a fluffy cardi. Mum said so.'

'She made it up.'

'Mum wouldn't do that.' She wouldn't. Mum never made stuff up.

'She would, to keep you safe.'

'Safe?' I stared at Grandma. 'Safe from what?'

Grandma shrugged. 'Snakes? Spiders? Marauding possums? You know what she's like, terrified of anything happening to you. You'd have insisted on going with her if she'd told you the truth.'

'Eh?' I had no idea what she was talking about.

'She's gone to look for your dad.'

My mouth dropped open and a bit of *Twinkle Flake* fell out. 'I know!' Grandma slapped her hand on the table. 'Did you ever hear anything so ridiculous? Your mum's got no search and rescue skills whatsoever. What's she going to do if she meets a **CROC**?

Carry out a risk assessment? Give it a lecture? Knit it a hat?'

My mouth was still open. I couldn't believe it. Mum? Looking for Dad? Why hadn't she said?

Grandma shook her head. 'I offered to go with her, but she wasn't having it. She wouldn't give me any of the details. **She was very rude, in fact.** She said if I went, something would be bound to go wrong. She said we'd probably be arrested for wombat smuggling! How ridiculous, Ollie. I haven't been caught smuggling in years. I shouldn't have taken any notice of her.' She tutted. 'I'd have much more chance of finding your dad than she would.'

I wasn't so sure about that, but I was still reeling. 'Why does she think he crashed in Australia?' I said. 'How does she know where to look?'

Grandma brandished the piece of paper. 'Here. Read this. Your mum hid it in her desk drawer. No idea how it ended up in my bag. **No idea at all.**'

It was an email. Addressed to Mum.

My dearest Mrs Brown,

I do hope you don't mind me contacting you.

I own a small, yet charming hotel in Humpty Doo – a town just to the east of Darwin. As you can imagine, I'm a busy chap. It was only today I picked up an old newspaper and discovered that your husband – the famous explorer, Henry Brown – is missing.

The news brought to mind an incident three weeks ago, when I was out on a crocodile hunt. A small plane flew overhead. Shortly after, I heard a distant thud.

After reading the article I am convinced it was your husband's plane I saw. I estimate he crashed around ten miles from here. The Australian bush is hazardous, as you know, but there is every chance a search party could find him alive. I have asked Darwin TV to appeal for volunteers.

I think it would draw attention to the cause if you and your son, Oliver, came to Australia to help with the search. You would be more than welcome to stay at Humpty Doo Towers (at a reduced rate, of course)

I look forward to hearing from you.

Yours sincerely
Mr Bruce Loops, Esq.

My mouth fell open again. I couldn't believe it! This was **much worse** than Mum just not taking me to Clacton! **MUM HAD GONE TO AUSTRALIA.** She'd made a load of stuff up. She'd lied to me. How could she? I had as much right as her to go looking for Dad! I'd even been invited!

I handed the email back and stood up. 'I'll go and find my passport,' I said. 'And then I'm going to pack.'

Grandma sprang to her feet. 'I'll ring the airline, Ollie. Then I'll call Bruce and let him know we're on our way.'

10

'**EIGHT THOUSAND POUNDS?**' Grandma screeched. 'Eight thousand pounds for two seats on a plane?' She slammed the study door behind her. 'And that's not even for first class, with complimentary nuts.' She stomped back into the kitchen. 'It's outrageous, Ollie. **Outrageous.**'

'I could write a letter of complaint,' I offered. 'Mum sometimes does that and gets free stuff. Once she got a pasty.'

'Not enough time. We'll have to raise the money somehow. What can we sell?'

'I don't think we've got anything very valuable,' I said. 'Dad's plane cost a lot. What about Mum's trophy?'

'Plastic,' said Gran. 'They wouldn't have wanted it to topple and crush anyone.'

I looked around. There were a couple of china rabbits on the window ledge but I'd won those at an amusement arcade in Swanage and was pretty sure they weren't worth anything. I had loads of football cards and Mum was always moaning about how much those cost, but I didn't think she'd spent as much as eight thousand on them.

Then I noticed Rose. He'd got down from the table and was prancing about in front of the mirror again. He seemed to like his pink bows. Every now and then, he'd yap admiringly at himself.

'Grandma,' I said. 'There's a **reward** for Rose. I mean, you probably shouldn't claim a reward for something you've stolen in the first place, but I could ring Bert, you know – **anonymously** – and see how much it is?'

'Return him to those thugs?' Grandma snatched Rose up and cradled him in her arms. 'How could you, Ollie? Look at his dear little face. We'll have to think of something else.'

Rose's face didn't look that dear to me. 'But, Grandma,' I argued, **'if it's a choice between Rose and finding Dad then surely —'**

'Hi,' said Piper. She walked into the kitchen. 'The front door was unlocked so I let myself in.'

'Why aren't you at school?' I asked.

'Everyone's panicking about catching your scarlet fever,' said Piper. 'So when I said I'd seen you yesterday, Mrs Jones went green with fright and said I must be incubating. I'm not allowed back for three weeks! How are you feeling, Ollie? You don't look very ill to me.'

'I'm fine, thanks,' I said, fake coughing.

'I wouldn't bother with the reward. It's not very much.'

Grandma spun around. 'How do you know?' she said.

'Oh,' said Piper. 'I phoned Bert last night.'

'You did WHAT?'

'Don't worry. I didn't tell him anything. I just wanted to find out how much it was. It's only a measly twenty-five quid. I wasn't going to grass you up for that.'

'How kind of you,' I said. 'Thanks a bunch.'

'Twenty-five quid?' said Grandma. 'See? That proves they don't want him back. Now come on, Ollie, tell Piper about our trip. Maybe she can help raise some money.'

Piper was very keen to help. **Piper was also very keen to come to Australia with us.** 'I'll be an asset,' she kept saying. 'I can map-read and carry stuff. Mum won't mind. Not if I'm incubating. And if your dad's stuck in a swamp it'll need two of us to keep his head above water while the other one runs for help.'

Grandma thought Piper coming with us was an excellent idea. My opinion was not asked for. If it had been, then Piper would **definitely** not be coming with us.

Grandma said we should have a meeting, which sounded like a good idea. 'Ollie?' she said. 'You're in charge of pens. Piper? You're in charge of squash.'

'What are you in charge of?' I asked.

'Writing stuff down. Come on. We need twelve thousand pounds by tomorrow.'

'How about a talent show?' Piper lifted Rose on to her lap. 'We could charge everyone ten quid to enter. Obviously, we'd put "Grand Prize" on the posters, but not say it was only a Mars Bar.'

'That's rubbish,' I said. 'We'd need to have one thousand, two hundred contestants.'

'Gosh, anyone would think you were going to be an accountant.' Piper pulled a face. 'How about you shave your head? I'd give a fiver to see that, and I bet everyone else at school would.'

'Or we could lock you in a tank full of **rats** for twenty-four hours?'

'I wouldn't mind,' said Piper. 'I like rats.'

'You would.'

'An excellent idea,' Grandma said, scribbling it down. 'Anything else?'

'A garage sale?' Piper said.

'Fantastic!' said Grandma. 'Whose garage shall we sell?'

'You don't sell anyone's garage,' I said. 'It's like a jumble sale. You just sell old stuff.'

'That's a shame,' said Grandma. 'A whole garage would have raised a lot of money. Especially yours, Ollie, it's massive.'

'Is that where your dad built his plane?' asked Piper.

I nodded.

'Is there anything worth selling in it?'

'I shouldn't think so,' I said. 'We could have a look later.'

Piper got up and walked over to the window. She stared out. She had Rose over her shoulder, and was patting his back, like a baby.

'Aren't you supposed to be in charge of squash,

Piper?' I said. 'I'm a bit thirsty.'

'I thought I heard your gate.'

'Probably the wind,' said Grandma. 'Now, Ollie, come on. You're the brainy one. Your mum's always posting your certificates on Facebook.'

'Ollie's only **average**,' Piper said. 'I beat him by miles in the last maths test.'

'Well, you're hardly top of the class, Piper,' I said. 'Remember that time Mrs Jones "forgot her glasses"? She hadn't. She just couldn't read your awful handwriting.'

'You can say all the nasty things you want, Ollie,' said Piper. 'But every time you do, I shall think about that school trip when you fell flat on your face in a **COWPAT**.'

'Did you, Ollie? A **COWPAT?**' Grandma snorted. 'How funny! Your mum didn't put that online. Did you manage to get a photo, Piper? I'd like to see it.'

'I think,' I said, as coldly as I could, 'we need to get on with this meeting.'

'Quite right, Ollie,' said Piper. 'What's your next idea? Oh, that's right. **You haven't had any.**'

'I haven't noticed you coming up with anything that isn't stupid,' I said.

Piper shrugged. 'Well, at least I'm trying – and it's **your** dad we're rescuing. Can I borrow your laptop?' she asked Grandma.

'Of course,' Grandma said, pushing it across the table. 'Do you need any help with it, dear? The "on" button's on the top, yes, that's right, just there, and then that little—'

'It's OK,' said Piper. 'I've used one before. Oh. Where's Rose going?'

'He needs to do his business,' Grandma said. 'I'll take him out. You two carry on.'

I tried to see what Piper was looking at on the computer. 'Don't tell me you've come up with something?' I said. 'What are you googling?'

Piper hunched over the screen so I couldn't see it. 'Just stuff,' she said. She tapped at the keys.

'What stuff?' I got up and walked around behind her. I didn't trust Piper. I peered over her shoulder. 'Why are you searching for Choodle?' I asked.

'I'm going to see how much Rose is worth,' Piper said. **'I think we should sell him.'**

'Grandma won't let you,' I said.

'This is a life or death situation, Ollie. Your gran can always get another dog – a cheaper one.'

'I guess,' I said.

'Blimey,' said Piper. 'Look at this.' She spun the laptop round.

'What?'

'Just read it,' Piper said.

Rose, according to Wikipedia, is not just any old Egyptian Choodle.

He is the only Egyptian Choodle in the world.
The last of his line.

HE IS A THREE THOUSAND-YEAR-OLD DOG OF DESTINY.

A teller of fortune. A bringer of luck.

He is not worth millions.

HE IS PRICELESS.

'And look at this bit,' Piper said, giggling.

I read it out.

"The Dog of Destiny belongs to no one, and goes only where he chooses. He is guided though life by fate, allowing events to unfurl around him. On occasions, he may choose to use his skills to assist the unfurling of those events."

'What does that mean, exactly?' Piper said.

'It's suggesting,' I said, 'that he can make things happen.'

'What?' said Piper. 'If you believe that, you're dumber than I thought. We're not at Hogwarts, Ollie. Dogs aren't magic.'

'I didn't say I believed it, Piper, but if you read it, instead of just looking at the pictures, you'd be able to see that:

"Twenty-first century scientists think the Dog of Destiny uses a combination of intuition and animal telepathy to make judgements about his surroundings, and uses his intelligence to help other mammals make positive decisions."'

'Right,' said Piper. 'Ha ha.'

I ignored her. 'It goes on to say that:

"They have no explanation for the lucky aura that surrounds the dog, and cannot say how he is seemingly immortal."'

Piper rolled her eyes. 'Of course he's not **immortal**. Nothing is. He'll have been replaced. It's like hamsters, isn't it?'

'What do you mean?'

'Well, hamsters only live for about five minutes, don't they? In our house, every time one pops off, Mum nips out and buys a replacement. My brother thinks his hamster's four! Imagine!'

'My hamster's six,' I said. 'Mum says she's never known a hamster live so long, and it must be because I look after her so well.'

'That must be it, Ollie, because—'

'Hey,' I said. 'Have you seen this bit?

"Those who treat the dog with care and respect can shortly expect an increase of their fortune, the return of lost belongings – and, on occasion, the granting of their heart's desire."'

I looked at Piper. 'That must have been why Bert and Ed bought all those scratch cards at the service station. They must have been hoping to win something.'

'I bet they're **furious** your gran pinched him,' Piper said.

I felt a bit nervous. Suppose they'd followed us home from the shop? I heard a noise in the hallway. 'What's that?' I said.

Piper smirked. 'I think your gran and Wonder Dog are back.'

Rose trotted into the kitchen. Blimey. I couldn't imagine him granting anyone's heart's desire. One of his bows had come undone, and Grandma had re-tied it around his tail. He didn't look like a rare dog of destiny. He looked like a bit of a **twit**.

Grandma bustled in after him. 'Rose has been terribly good, he did his business twice and neither time on your mum's lawn.' She came over and sat down. 'What have I missed?'

'Did you know?' asked Piper.

'Know what, dear?'

'About Rose?'

'About Rose? What about Rose?' She picked up her pen. 'Shall we get on?'

'That he's supposed to be lucky?' I said.

'I don't know what you're talking about,' Grandma said. 'I rescued a little dog from being badly treated. That's all. I had **absolutely no idea** he was a priceless dog of destiny. No idea **whatsoever**. That's not why I stole him, **certainly** not.'

We looked at her.

Grandma scowled. 'Oh, all right then,' she said. 'I did know.'

'Bert and Ed weren't being mean to him?'

'Not really.'

'Honestly, Grandma,' I said. 'What were you thinking?'

'I needed him more than they did.' Grandma looked sulky.

'What for?' Piper asked.

Grandma mumbled something.

'Pardon?' I said.

'Oh, Ollie.' Grandma dabbed her eye. 'I've never taken any notice of your mum before. I should be the one searching for your dad. It's what I do. But, before I knew it, I'd agreed to stay here and babysit you instead. What was I thinking?'

'Well, sorry for being an inconvenience,' I said.

'It's not that. Those rhinos didn't just take my leg, Ollie, **they took my confidence**.'

'Oh,' I said. Blimey. This was heavy stuff. Maybe I should get her a Jaffa Cake?

'So yesterday, when I saw Rose at the service station, I could hardly believe my eyes! It was meant to be, Ollie, it was **fate!**'

I stared at Grandma. She didn't really believe Rose was anything other than a small, scruffy dog, did she?

'You know how fond I am of rare and precious things,' she went on. 'I'd heard about the Dog

81

of Destiny – he's legendary in explorer circles, but I never thought he existed. Did you read the Wikipedia page? He's a finder of lost things! **A bringer of luck!'** She clapped her hands in excitement. 'Now we have Rose, Ollie, we can't fail to bring your dad home safely.'

'Right,' I said.

Grandma tutted. 'See? That's why I didn't tell you. I knew you'd scoff.'

I looked down at Rose. He was under the table having a vigorous scratch. **'He's a dog,'** I said. **'How can a dog have powers?'**

'Wait and see. He's come to help in our hour of need. He'll be casting his lucky aura all over us. You believe in him, don't you, Piper?'

'Um ... definitely,' Piper looked like she was trying not to laugh.

'And you should too, Ollie.' Grandma tapped the table sternly. **'As far as I can see, he's the best chance we've got of getting your dad home.'**

I raised my eyebrows. I was going to find it really hard to believe in a lucky dog. 'OK,' I said. 'I'll try.'

'Hey!' Piper suddenly turned. 'Did you hear that?'

'Hear what?'

'Outside.'

'I didn't hear anything,' I said.

Rose stopped scratching.

THE DOORBELL RANG.

'Quick,' said Grandma. 'Hide.' She picked up Rose and shoved him under her cardigan. 'Piper, get behind the sofa.'

'What about me?' I tried to squeeze in after them. 'Move up, Piper, you're taking all the room.'

'Not you, Ollie. You go and answer the door,' Grandma said. She gave me a shove.

'Me? Why me?' That was a bit unfair!

'Because you live here, and you haven't recently stolen a dog.'

'I guess,' I said. I crawled back out.

'Now, if it's someone from the school, keep

coughing without putting your hand over your mouth – that'll get rid of them.'

'OK,' I said.

'If it's that awful woman from next door, tell her that Rose and I had **absolutely nothing** to do with the little poos on her front lawn.'

'Right,' I said.

'If it's Bert and Ed – it won't be – tell them you saw a small magical dog ambling by himself in the park, just this morning.'

'OK,' I said, as I walked down the hall. I hoped it wasn't Bert and Ed.

I opened the door.

It was Bert and Ed.

12

I stepped out on to the path and pulled the door shut behind me. I didn't want Rose to run out, yapping.

'Can I help you?' I said, politely.

'Good morning, small boy,' said Ed. He was still wearing his scarf, but it wasn't wrapped around his face today. It was casually draped over his shoulders. Bert was behind him, holding a clipboard. He stepped forward. 'Is your mum in?' he asked.

I didn't tell him she was in Australia. I told him she was upstairs with a headache.

Ed said it didn't matter. 'We're doing a survey,' he said. 'All you have to do is answer some questions.'

'And in return, son,' Bert said, 'you can have one of these vouchers here, for a "Make Your Own Crisps" kit.' He waved a bit of paper at me.

'OK,' I said, even though I didn't really want a

'Make Your Own Crisps' kit. I just wanted them to go away.

'Here goes.' Ed cleared his throat and glanced at his hand. He had the questions written on it. 'One. Who lives in this delightful house here?'

'Just me, my mum and my dad.'

Ed looked disappointed.

'Only the three of you?'

'Yes.'

'No elderly relative? Long skirt? Limp? Bushy hair?'

'Definitely not,' I said.

Bert made a little dash on his paper. Ed looked at his hand again. 'Question two. Does anyone in this house own a **Mini?'**

I checked to make sure Grandma's car was still hidden in the hedge. 'Nope,' I said.

'Any pets? Cat? Mouse? <u>Dear little doggy?</u>'

'Just a hamster,' I said. 'Myrtle.'

Bert nodded and made another mark. 'Hamster, eh?' he said. 'Splendid pets, but they don't last five minutes, do they? Shame.'

'Myrtle was six last week, actually,' I said.

Ed sniggered. 'Six?' he said. 'That's a pretty old hamster. Is it one of those **"SPECIAL"** hamsters whose fur turns a slightly different shade every few months?'

'Mum says all hamsters change colour every now and then,' I said. 'What's the next question? I'm quite busy this morning.'

Ed scowled. 'Question four. Have you noticed anyone around here being "lucky" over the last twenty-four hours? A neighbour winning the lottery? Taking home the sweetie hamper from the school fair?'

'No,' I said. 'I haven't heard of anyone being lucky.'

Bert and Ed looked disappointed. Bert tucked the clipboard under his arm. 'Well. Thanks for your help. Here's your voucher. Give that number a call and they'll send you a potato.'

'Thanks,' I said, as they walked off down the path. I shut the door and locked it, and then I put the chain on.

'Can we come out?' Grandma's voice whispered, as I walked back in. 'I don't want to be rude about your mother's housekeeping skills, but there's a shocking amount of dust behind here. Poor Rose has been sneezing and sneezing **and then he accidentally farted** and that's made poor Piper feel terribly sick. Ollie? Is it safe?

'Better wait a minute,' I whispered back, even though Bert and Ed had already let themselves out the gate. I'd let Piper suffer a bit longer.

Grandma popped her head out. 'You didn't tell them anything, did you?'

'No,' I said. 'But they're not happy.'

'Naturally,' said Grandma. 'They wanted to win themselves a load of cash.' She handed me Rose and pulled herself all the way out. 'Not like us. We need him for **NOBLE** causes.'

'We could do with some, though.' Piper clambered after Grandma. 'For the tickets.'

Grandma looked at me. 'Do you think that would be all right, Ollie? To harness his powers for monetary gain?'

I looked down at Rose. **There was no way he was lucky.**

'I'm sure that would be absolutely fine,' I said.

13

Once Piper had stopped feeling sick we carried on with the meeting. I was doing a great job with the pens, but Piper still hadn't made any squash.

'What happens if they come back?' Piper asked. 'Or go to the 𝕡𝕠𝕝𝕚𝕔𝕖?'

'Ha, they won't go to the police,' Grandma said. 'They probably stole him themselves. Do you think they've gone, Ollie? I have an idea, but it involves leaving the house. If they're hanging about, they're bound to recognise me.'

'I think I convinced them we only had a hamster,' I said. 'I did a pretty good job.'

'Wear something different,' said Piper to Grandma. 'How about a **hat**?'

'Of course!' Grandma looked delighted. 'Why didn't I think of that? Ollie, are there any in the dressing-up box?'

'There's a fez,' I said. 'Or I've got a balaclava.'

'I'm not sure either of those would be suitable,' Grandma said. 'I don't want to draw attention to myself.'

'Why don't you borrow one of Ollie's mum's dresses?' Piper suggested.

'Piper. You're a genius.' Grandma looked delighted. She shoved Rose on to my lap and ran out the room.

I didn't know if that was such a good idea. Grandma was a lot bigger than Mum. 'Do you think we should go up?' I said. 'She might get stuck in something.'

'She'll be fine,' said Piper. 'Have you got any plasticine?'

'There's some in the cupboard,' I said. 'What's it for?'

'I'll make your gran a **false nose**. Not a massive one – her nose is big enough already, but we could change the shape a bit.'

'Won't it fall off?'

'We'll use superglue,' said Piper. 'Oh wow. You look amazing, Ollie's gran.'

'Do you think?' Grandma gave a twirl. She'd chosen one of Mum's 'special occasion' dresses, which was a bright shiny pink and had purple flowers all over it.

'It looked different on Mum,' I said.

'It was too long before. I cut a bit off.'

'I made you a nose.' Piper held it out. 'It's not quite the right shade, but I think it'll do.'

'Superb, Piper. Thank you.'

'What's your idea?' I asked.

'We'll need some cash,' said Grandma. 'Ollie – get the emergency tin out of the cupboard.'

'It's empty,' I said. 'We bought biscuits, remember?'

'Wasn't there any change?'

'Three pounds,' I said.

'It'll do,' said Grandma. 'We're going to that casino at the end of the high street. We'll stick it on red and **let it ride**.'

'Eh?' Piper looked up at her. 'Let it ride on what?'

'Mum would be really cross if I got bucked off anything,' I said.

'Haven't you heard of roulette?' Grandma tutted. 'What do they teach you at school? It's a board game, and **perfectly safe**. You choose between black and red. Then you spin a ball in a wheel. If the ball lands on the colour you've picked, you double your money!'

'OK,' said Piper. 'So if we put three pounds on black and the ball lands on black – we end up with six pounds?'

'Exactly right!' said Grandma.

'Well, it's certainly worth making the trip for six pounds,' said Piper. 'That's pretty close to the twelve thousand we need.'

'As I said – we'll let it ride.' Grandma grabbed her bag from the back of the chair. 'That means we leave our money on the table for twelve spins. As long as we win every time – well, you work it out.'

I started adding it up in my head, but show-off Piper got in first. 'We'll have twelve thousand, two hundred and eighty-eight pounds,' she said. 'That's loads!'

'Suppose we lose?' I said.

'We won't,' said Grandma, giving Rose a pat before shoving him in her bag. 'We've got a lucky dog. **We can't possibly lose.**'

14

As we walked down to the high street I noticed a few people giving Grandma odd looks. I wasn't surprised, as Great Potton is stuffed with people who only wear beige. I don't know who invented beige but I hope they're sorry about it. It's a really miserable colour. Sometimes, when people want to sell you beige stuff, they try to fool you by calling it 'toffee' or 'buff' (which actually means 'naked', ha ha), but, at the end of the day, beige is the colour of pastry and old people's coats.

Grandma wasn't beige though. Grandma was pink and purple and wearing a false nose and striding down the street on her squeaky leg clutching an enormous handbag which had the **rarest dog in the world** inside. Grandma could never be beige.

'Here we are.' She stopped and looked up.

'Great Potton Casino!'

Great Potton Casino didn't look anything like the casinos I'd seen in films. I couldn't see any palm trees. I looked around for golden pillars and statues and dishes full of pineapples but all I could see were some concrete steps leading up to a dark passageway, and a frayed red rope hooked between two posts.

Standing behind the rope was a man wearing a black suit. He didn't look very friendly.

'Excuse me,' said Grandma. 'Is this the way to the roulette?'

The man looked her up and down. Then he looked at me and Piper.

'Ha,' he said. 'You're kidding me, right?'

'I beg your pardon?'

The man pointed at me and Piper. 'You have to be **TWENTY-ONE** to come in here. They're about eight.'

I'm eleven! I was just about to say so when Grandma gave me a shove.

'We're a school visit,' she said. 'I booked ages ago.'

'A school visit?' The man looked confused. 'Do we do those?'

'Gambling.' Grandma nodded. 'It's a compulsory part of the new PSHE syllabus. Government funded.'

The man looked a bit doubtful, but even so, he unhooked the rope and waved us through. 'Get your chips on the way in. One pound minimum bet, ten thousand max. All drinks fifteen pounds each.'

'Make sure you ask for tap water,' hissed Grandma, as we walked down the corridor. 'They're not allowed to charge for that.'

Piper sniffed the air. 'Where do we get the chips?' she asked.

'They're not **CHIP** chips, dear,' Grandma said. 'They're plastic tokens to use on the roulette table. Ah, here we are. Give the lady our money, Ollie.'

The woman behind the glass window looked suspicious. 'Are you twenty-one?' she asked.

'We're a school visit,' I said.

'Really?'

'Yep,' I said. 'Great Potton Primary.'

'How lovely! Three pounds? Is that it? Don't lose it all at once. There you go. Three chips.'

'Three?' said Piper. 'Is that all we get?'

'It's all we need.' Grandma patted her bag. 'Don't forget, Piper, we have Rose. Come on, it's this way.'

We walked through some double doors into a room that was stuffy and dark. Nothing was made of marble and my feet stuck to the carpet. A blonde girl leant against a table in the middle of the room. As we walked over the she raised her eyebrows and smirked, but she didn't say we couldn't play.

'Is that a fruit bowl?' I asked. I couldn't see any pineapples in it.

'It's the roulette wheel,' the girl said. She looked like she was trying not to laugh. How rude! It had looked like a fruit bowl to me. I'd thought there might have been pineapples in it.

'Place your bets, ladies and gentleman.' The girl wasn't even trying not to laugh now. We'd show her!

This place would have to shut after we'd won all their money!

'Come on then,' said Grandma. 'What colour shall we choose for our first spin? Red or black?'

'Black,' I said.

Piper giggled. 'Maybe you should ask the magical mutt of mystery?' she said.

'Good idea.' Grandma opened her bag. 'What do you think, Ros— Oh. He's asleep. Never mind. I expect his lucky aura is pulsating all around us. Go ahead – put it on black, Ollie. I've got a good feeling.'

I put our three chips on the black square. This was so exciting! I was pretty sure Rose didn't have a lucky aura, but even so, we had an excellent chance of winning! I noticed Piper had her fingers crossed, so I crossed mine too.

In as little as ten minutes we could have our twelve thousand pounds!

The girl spun the fruit bowl. Then she picked up a tiny silver ball and threw it in. I could see it shooting round and round and I held my breath. This was it! We were going to win! It was so exciting! I looked across at Grandma. She'd get her false nose caught if she leant over any further. 'Black,' I could hear her muttering. 'Black black black black.'

The wheel was a blur. I tried to focus on the section the ball had landed in. **Black black black BLACK!** I was sure it was black!

The wheel was slowing. Yay! It was black! **WOO HOO!** Maybe Rose was lucky after all?

The wheel stopped.

Oh.

It wasn't black.

It was red.

'Bad luck, guys.' The girl reached out with a little rake thing and pulled our chips towards her.

'Want to play again?'

'Hang on a minute,' said Grandma. 'Wasn't that our practice go?'

'Practice go?' said the girl. 'I'm afraid we don't do practice goes.'

'I'm sure you do for school visits.' Grandma gave her a winning smile.

'No, we don't. Now – any more bets?'

'How can we?' said Grandma. 'You've taken our money.'

'Um – that's because you **lost**,' said the girl. She pressed a little bell on the edge of the table. I didn't like her.

'You couldn't have spun it properly,' I said.

'I'd be quiet if I were you,' said the girl. 'You were the one who said "black".'

'Yeah, Ollie,' said Piper, accusingly.

That's right, blame me.

'Did you call security, Ruby?' The man from outside walked up behind us.

'That girl took our money,' said Grandma, as he propelled us towards the double doors. 'She said we could have a practice go, and then she took our money. I'll be writing to the *Guardian*.'

'Hang on,' called the girl. 'Is this yours?' She was holding up something pink and strange-looking.

'Your nose fell off, Grandma,' I said.

'They took our money,' Grandma muttered as we walked up to the town square. 'Crooks. The lot of them.'

'She didn't actually say we could have a practice go,' I said, as we sat on the wall that went round the fountain. 'You made that up.'

Grandma was trying to squish her nose back on, but it wouldn't stick so she popped it down beside her. She looked into her bag and sighed. 'Rose is still asleep,' she said. 'Maybe I should have woken him up? Perhaps he's only lucky when he's awake?'

'Or maybe he's just a regular dog?' I muttered under my breath.

'Don't forget to believe, Ollie,' said Piper. I could see her smirking out of the corner of my eye. I scowled at her. I wished she'd go home. We hadn't won enough money to buy a scratch card, let alone the plane tickets. We'd never find Dad – and Mum would probably get lost trying to find him. <u>**FOR ALL I KNEW, I WAS ALREADY AN ORPHAN.**</u>

'Cheer up,' said Grandma. 'What's wrong?'

'I'm worried about Mum,' I said. 'There are loads of dangerous animals in Australia.'

'Don't be silly,' Grandma said. 'Your mum's still on the plane. She can't possibly be eaten by anything till she gets there.'

'Thanks,' I said. 'I feel much better now.'

Piper had taken her shoes and socks off and was splashing around behind us.

'Would you mind not doing that?' I said.

'There's loads of money in here,' she said. 'People throw it in for luck.'

'I hope you're not thinking of stealing any,' I said.

'It'd be for a good cause,' she said. 'Anyone would think you didn't want to find your dad.'

I stood up. **How dare she say that!**

'I'm going home.' I said.

'You've sat in something,' said Piper.

'It's my nose,' said Grandma. 'Ha ha. Look at your trousers.'

I didn't care about my trousers. I just wanted to get to Australia. As soon as we got home I was going to call another meeting. If Rose did have any powers he'd better start using them soon. If he didn't, we'd have to sell him. Grandma wouldn't like it but I couldn't see any other way of helping Dad.

'Are you lot coming?' I started walking away.

Then I stopped.

There were two men standing outside Boots.

I took a step backwards. 'Grandma,' I hissed, **'it's Bert and Ed.'**

Too late. They'd seen us.

'Hey,' Bert said. He started walking over. 'Aren't you the lady that took our dog?'

'Pardon?' Grandma tried to cover her bag with her skirt, but it was too short. 'Did you say I took your

105

dog? I haven't got a dog. How could I take your dog if I haven't got one? I mean, if I had a dog, then fair enough. Accuse away. But I haven't. Look. No dog.'

'What's that in your bag, then?' asked Bert.

'My bag?' Grandma reached down and shoved Rose's head back in. 'That's not a dog. It's a guinea pig. She just won Best Guinea Pig in Show at the Town Hall.'

'It can't have won Best Guinea Pig,' said Ed. 'It's a dog.'

Grandma stood up. 'It's a guinea pig. Come on, Ollie. Come on, Piper. Time to get Gerty home. If you wouldn't mind, gentlemen.' She strode forward and elbowed them aside.

I swear we almost got away with it, but Rose popped his head back out and **started yapping**.

We ran round the fountain three times one way, and then the other way. We pounded up the high street into WH Smith and out the back entrance to the multi-storey car park.

'Come on, Piper,' I shouted over my shoulder. **'Stop being so slow.'**

'Into the lift,' puffed Grandma. 'The doors are open.'

'What about Piper?' I asked.

'She'll have to take the stairs,' said Grandma. She pressed the button. Nothing happened. She pressed it again. 'It's your bum, Ollie. It's in the way of the doors. Move it.'

'It's not my bum,' I said. I squished into the lift a bit more. 'We should wait for Piper. Suppose Bert and Ed catch her?'

'They want Rose, not a small ginger child,' said Grandma. 'I think this lift is broken.'

'Hi there,' Piper said as she strolled up. 'What's the rush?'

I stuck my head out. There was no sign of Bert and

Ed. 'Didn't they follow us?' I asked.

'No,' Piper said. 'They know where you live, Ollie. They wandered off in that direction.'

'So let me get this right,' I said. 'We've lost all our money because of a lucky dog that actually isn't, and Bert and Ed are out to get us? **Well, that's just great then, isn't it?'**

Grandma covered Rose's ears. 'Ollie! Don't be rude about Rose. We've been expecting him to know what we want. Maybe we need to tell him?'

'And don't worry about Bert and Ed,' Piper said. 'I sorted that.'

'Really, Piper? How?' Grandma looked impressed.

'I called the police station and told them there were two thugs hanging about outside your house. They're sending someone now.'

'Oh, well done!' said Grandma. 'You're so clever.'

As we turned into our street, a police car shot past with Bert and Ed sitting in the back. They looked furious.

'How long do you think we've got?' Piper said as we let ourselves in. 'They're bound to come back.'

'We'll take precautions,' Grandma said. 'Keep the door locked at all times.'

'I'll draw the curtains,' said Piper.

I put a note out that said **'no milk for two weeks'**. I thought that was pretty good. It looked like we'd gone on holiday.

'Rose is going curly again.' Grandma put him down on his cushion. 'I'd better get the straighteners out.'

'I wouldn't bother,' said Piper. 'They didn't fall for the disguise. You may as well change his name back.'

'I think he prefers Rose,' said Grandma. She twirled his bunches. 'It must be nice to have a change after three thousand years. Ollie, get his dinner, will you? He needs to keep his strength up.'

'Yes. It must be terribly tiring being so lucky,' I said. I opened the cupboard and took out the last tin of Small Dog's Delight. Piper handed me the opener.

'Don't forget to check the lid for the golden bone,'

she said. 'You never know.'

'Oh! The competition!' Grandma raced over. 'I bet we've won!'

'I bet we haven't,' I said. 'It's not like Rose was at the shop, choosing the tins.'

'Wait, Ollie. I'll get him.' She dashed over and grabbed Rose. 'Now, Rose. **Cast your lucky aura.**'

'He's quivering,' said Piper. 'Do you think that means anything?'

'He's probably hungry,' I said.

'I have such a good feeling about this,' said Grandma. She shuffled even closer. 'Budge up, will you, Piper, I can't see.'

'Standing so close,' I said, 'won't make a golden bone appear.' I elbowed her away a bit, and used the end of the tin opener to pry the lid all the way open.

'Quick, wipe off the jelly,' said Grandma. Her nose was practically in it. 'I'm sure I see a glint of gold. This is it! This is it!'

Ugh. It was disgusting. It smelt all meaty.

We stared at the cleaned-off lid.

It wasn't 'it'.

There was no golden bone.

There wasn't even a 'Sorry, you are not a winner on this occasion'.

We had won ZILCH.

ZERO.

ZIP.

16

'**Never mind.**' **Grandma** scraped the food into a bowl. 'We were probably expecting far too much. I mean, there's luck, and then there's luck.'

'What's the difference?' I watched Rose scoffing his dinner. 'Either he's lucky or he's not.'

'What happened to the other tin?' Piper asked. 'You bought two, didn't you?

'Rose had it for breakfast.' I looked at Grandma. 'Did you check it?'

'No! I didn't! I threw it away.' Grandma made a leap for the bin. She pulled out the bag and tipped it on to the floor. 'Help me look.'

Rose came over to watch us root through the rubbish.

'Didn't Mum make these?' I asked. I held up a nut cutlet.

'I was making room in the freezer for ice cream,' Grandma explained. 'I didn't think you'd mind. They call it collateral damage.'

'There it is!' Piper grabbed a tin. 'The lid's missing,' she said. 'Keep looking.'

'Oh!' Grandma gave a little cry and pointed at Rose. 'No need!' She clapped excitedly. **'He's found it!** It's in his mouth! What a **clever** boy.'

'Oh wow!' said Piper. 'Well done, Rose!'

Rose trotted over to Piper and dropped the lid at her feet. She scooped it up and peered closely at both sides.

'We've won, haven't we?' Grandma clasped her hands eagerly.

Piper threw the lid back into the pile. 'Nope.'

I was really annoyed. For a moment there, I'd almost believed in magical dogs. I gave Rose a glare and then sat and looked at the mess. Perhaps I should just go back to school? It'd be one less thing for Mum to be mad about when she got home.

113

'Ollie?'

'What?'

Piper was staring over at the tin sitting on the worktop. The one I'd just opened.

'It's upside down,' she said.

'Eh?' Oh. She was right.

The lid hadn't been the lid. The lid was at the bottom.

We were over there in seconds. Piper grabbed it. She held it to her eye.

'Oh my God,' she said.

'Ha ha,' I said. 'Funny.'

'No! Look.' She held it out.

'I'm not falling for it, Piper.'

She passed the tin to

Grandma instead.

WE'VE WON.

17

Grandma didn't hang around. We had our winnings by two o'clock.

'The man at Small Dog's Delight looked ever so surprised,' she said, emptying a pile of notes on to the table. 'He said he's been working there for forty years, and they've never had to give a prize away before. Imagine!' She gave Rose a pat.

'It's funny, isn't it?' said Piper. 'Twenty thousand sounds like loads, but it fits into one small bag.'

'It's all here.' Grandma finished counting it. 'So that's twelve thousand for the tickets.' She made one pile. 'And eight thousand for snacks and sundries.' She made another.

I wasn't sure what sundries were. They must be very expensive.

Grandma got straight on the phone to the airline.

'That's right,' she said. 'Three tickets for humans and one for a dog. Four in total.' She put her hand over the receiver. 'They've gone to see about Rose's ticket. I expect it's cheaper for him, he's so tiny, after all.'

'They'll probably put him in the hold, in a basket,' said Piper. 'At least the plane won't crash – not with a lucky dog on board.'

'Actually,' I said, 'flying is the safest way to travel, regardless of whether you have a lucky dog or not.'

'That's right,' said Piper. 'Unless, of course, you build your own plane, and the propeller drops off over a swamp.'

Did she think that was funny? I turned my back on her.

'Sorry,' Piper said. 'You were being a know-all.'

'Even so,' I said.

Grandma flapped her hand and shushed us. She pressed the phone hard against her ear. 'I beg your pardon?' she said. 'Did I just hear you say dogs have to go into quarantine? **Six months? That's ridiculous!**

We're only going for two weeks.' Her voice started to get screechy. **'It's Australia,'** she said. **'A country stuffed with poisonous snakes and germy old koalas – and you are worried about a dog?'**

It wasn't sounding good.

'What about a guinea pig?' Would you let a guinea pig in? Long haired? Cute?'

It didn't seem like guinea pigs were allowed into Australia either. Grandma looked like she might explode. 'In that case,' she said. 'If it's not too much trouble, I'll just take three human tickets. That's right. **HUMAN**. Definitely no dogs or guinea pigs.' She slammed down the receiver.

'Right,' she said. 'All sorted. We'll be in Australia by Wednesday.'

'Are we leaving Rose behind?' I said.

'No.' Grandma looked puzzled. 'Of course not.'

'I thought the airline said—'

'The airline said it would be perfectly fine to take Rose, as long as we don't let anyone see him.'

Grandma was lying again. 'I don't think they did say that,' I said.

Grandma ignored me. 'The flight's in three hours,' she said. 'We need to get on with it. Piper, you go home and get your passport and a change of clothes. Make sure you tell your mum where you're going, won't you?'

'I'll leave her a note,' said Piper. 'Shall I bring a swimming costume?'

'Definitely,' I said. 'There'll be loads of places you can have a dip, once you've checked for leeches.'

'I was thinking of the pool at Humpty Doo Towers, not the swamp, Ollie.' She gave a little hop. 'I can't wait,' she said. 'I've only ever stayed in a caravan before. This is going to be amazing.'

The airport was packed. Grandma said that was good as we wouldn't attract attention. She got her list out.

'Passports?'

'Yep,' said Piper.

'Tickets?'

'Yep.'

'Cuddly toy?'

'I don't see why I have to be the one to carry Rose,' I said.

Rose didn't like the bear costume Grandma had made. He'd stopped trying to bite it off, but he still looked pretty annoyed.

'He can't stay like that for the whole flight,' Piper said. 'What happens if he needs the loo?'

'We'll unzip him once we're in the air,' Grandma

said. 'It's only to get him through security. Ollie, stop looking so nervous.'

It was all very well for her to say that. **I could end up in jail.**

'You first, Piper,' said Grandma.

Piper was holding the boarding passes. She waltzed through the metal detectors and waved at us from the other side.

'Now it's your turn, Ollie. Go on. **I'll create a diversion.'** Grandma gave me a push.

I took a deep breath and walked towards the screens. I shouldn't have worried. None of the security guards were looking at me. They were all looking at Grandma, who was balanced on one leg and waving her false one about.

'What shall I do with this?' she bellowed. 'I wouldn't want to set your alarms off.'

A small boy behind her started to cry. Excellent.

I kept walking. I was past the security guards. I was through the screens. An alarm went off. Was that me? I glanced behind. No. It wasn't. Grandma's leg had jammed the X-ray. I was home and clear. I was good at this! I was great! I was cool as ice! I'd got away with it!

Then Rose barked.

'Shhhh,' I said.

One of the security guards looked over.

'Woof,' I said. 'Woof.'

Too late.

Grandma did a fantastic job of blaming me.

Piper did a fantastic job of rolling her eyes and looking like she couldn't believe anyone would be so stupid as to smuggle a dog on to a plane.

I did a fantastic job of pretending it was my idea

because I couldn't bear to leave my dog behind, and it definitely wasn't Piper and Grandma's fault, and that I was **very very VERY sorry**.

Rose just sat there scratching.

I got a telling off, but I didn't end up in jail, which was good.

They even gave us a refund on the tickets, which was also good.

I'll tell you what wasn't good. **Still being in Great Potton.**

19

'**Are you OK?**' Piper asked, as we were driving home from the airport.

'No,' I said.

It'd been her idea to dress Rose as a bear. I'd said all along we should hide him in the rucksack. Now look.

'Could you slow down, Grandma?' I asked. 'You're making me feel sick.'

'That's your mother's fault again,' Grandma said. 'This is regular driving. You're not used to it, that's all. How's Rose?'

Rose was sitting between me and Piper. He didn't look bothered we weren't on the plane. Well, why would he be? **It wasn't his dad that was missing!**

Grandma screeched on to our driveway. 'Come on. Let's get inside,' she said. 'We need an emergency meeting.'

123

'Good idea,' I said.

'Pizza or burgers?' Grandma said.

'Eh?'

'Let's get pizza,' Piper said. 'And fizzy pop. We can have it delivered.'

'Excuse me?' I blinked. Had they forgotten about Dad???

'I'll have ham and pineapple,' Piper said. 'I expect Rose would like pepperoni. What about you, Ollie's gran?

Grandma couldn't decide so she ordered **LOADS**. **Potton Pizza Palace had to send a van instead of their usual moped.**

'Having a party?' said the delivery man, as he handed them over.

'Nope,' I said. I kicked the door shut with a bang. It seemed to me that I was the only one taking this 'getting to Australia' thing seriously.

I shoved the pizzas on to the table. 'When,' I said, 'are we actually going to talk about what happens next?'

'Don't worry,' Grandma said. 'I already have a plan.'

'What is it?' I said.

'This? Cheese and tomato. Would you like a bit?' Grandma offered me the box.

I scowled. 'Not the pizza. Your plan. What is it?'

Grandma shrugged. 'I haven't thought of it yet. But I definitely have one. I'll let you know as soon as it comes to me.'

'Grandma.' I could feel myself getting upset. 'Mum and Dad could be in **terrible danger**, and – and ...' My voice cracked a little bit.

'Ollie.' Grandma reached over and patted my arm. 'Your dad's used to the wild. He's only lost! And Bruce will look after your mum. He sounded like a lovely man!'

'I just want to get out there as soon as possible,' I said. 'Do we have to take Rose?'

'Yes,' Grandma said. 'We do. Australia's a big place. Your dad could have wandered for miles. We need as much luck as we can get.'

'How about we post him?' Piper suggested.

'The post is dreadful. He wouldn't arrive till Christmas.' Grandma pushed aside her pizza crusts and stood up. 'Where's the key to your dad's workshop?'

'On the ledge above the door,' I said.

'**OMG**,' said Piper. 'Are you going to build us a plane? Overnight?'

My mouth dropped open. I hadn't thought of that! If Grandma could find the plans for Dad's plane, she could make another! That would be amazing!

'Don't be so silly,' Grandma said. 'I'm an explorer, not an engineer.'

'Why do you want the key, then?' I asked.

'I fancy a glass of home-brew,' Grandma said. 'That stuff your dad made? It's on those shelves at the back.'

'It's not any more,' I said. 'Mum threw it out. She thought it might fizz up. She said we'd had enough explosions for one year.'

'I wish your mother could let things go,' Grandma

complained. 'I'll have a look anyway. She might have missed a bottle.'

Rose had fallen asleep with his snout in his pizza. He looked worn out. I picked him up and put him on to his cushion. 'I'm going to bed,' I said to Piper. 'Are you staying here tonight?'

'Yep,' Piper said. 'I'll sleep on the sofa. I can raise the alarm if Bert and Ed turn up.'

'OK,' I said. 'See you in the morning.'

'Ollie?'

'What?'

'Don't worry. Your gran will think of something.'

20

I **had a** horrible dream about being attacked by a crocodile. It was just about to bite my head off when Mum appeared on roller-skates. She didn't look very pleased. 'This is all your gran's fault,' she said. 'Bet you wish you'd stayed at home.' Then she stabbed the crocodile with her knitting needle and there was a big explosion and bits went everywhere.

I was quite pleased when Grandma woke me up, though I could tell it wasn't morning as it was **still dark.**

She was standing at the end of my bed with her arms folded. She looked horribly serious. 'What's wrong?' I asked, sitting up.

'Your mother. That's what's wrong.'

'What's happened?' I jumped out of bed. 'Is she OK?'

'I'm sure she is,' Grandma said. 'I'm sure she's OK – apart from being a **BARE–FACED LIAR!**'

Eh? What was she on about? 'You mean all the stuff about Aunt Lucy?' I asked.

'No. Not the stuff about Aunt Lucy. That was an acceptable lie. This ... this is **unforgivable**.'

What on earth could Mum have done? Grandma was furious!

Piper appeared at the top of the stairs, blinking. 'You're making a lot of noise,' she said. She came into my room and switched on the light.

'Come in, Piper. Just listen to this. It's an OUTRAGE!'

'What is?'

Grandma was so cross she was practically purple. 'I let myself into your dad's workshop, you know, looking for the home-brew.

Well, like you said, there wasn't any, but I thought that while I was there, I'd have a quick check around.'

'And?' said Piper.

'You'll never believe what I found.'

'What?' I said.

Grandma shook her head. **'The deceit,'** she said.

'You're not making sense,' said Piper.

'I'd taken Rose with me, and he started sniffing at something. Something in the corner, under a cloth. It was quite large, so I thought maybe it was – oh, I don't know – a chest freezer or something. I thought there might be some ice cream in it – I'm very partial to Rocky Road – though for the life of me I can't understand why I got so excited. This is your mother we're talking about. What was I thinking? If it had been a chest freezer then it would have been filled with revolting home-made frozen yoghurt.'

'So it wasn't a freezer?'

'No, it was NOT.'

Piper and I looked at her expectantly.

She closed her eyes.

'**Oh, for goodness sake, Grandma,**' I said. '**What was it?**'

Grandma's eyes popped open. '**MY HOT-AIR BALLOON,**' she roared. '**MY HOT-AIR BALLOON THAT YOUR MUM TOLD ME HAD BEEN DAMAGED BEYOND REPAIR IN THE RHINO INCIDENT!**'

'Oh,' I said.

'When I think of that AWFUL car they bought me instead. The cheek of it.'

'I expect she was worried about you,' I said. 'You did lose a leg last time you went up in it.'

'I still have one left. Your mother had no right to make a decision like that. I loved my balloon.'

I'd never seen her look so mad. Mum was going to be in for it when she got home.

'It's OK, though?' asked Piper. 'Not damaged?'

'There's a small hole in the basket where the rhino stepped on it. Apart from that, it's absolutely fine.' Grandma stomped towards the door.

'Now get a move on, will you?'

I stared after her. Get a move on where? **It was the middle of the night, wasn't it?**

Piper grabbed my clothes and threw them at me. 'Come on.'

Eh?

'Hurry up,' Grandma shouted up the stairs. 'It won't get itself out.'

Oh. Right. I got it.

We were going to Australia.

BY BALLOON.

21

It took us a while to get everything out of the garage and into position. The basket was ever so heavy and a really awkward shape. By the time we'd fashioned a trolley out of the lawnmower and a plank, and wheeled everything into the garden, the sun was up.

Grandma bustled round telling everyone what to do.

I hammered four wooden pegs into the lawn and Piper attached the ropes from the basket. When she wasn't looking, I checked to make sure she'd done it **properly** (she doesn't go to Scouts like I do). One knot looked dodgy, so I retied it.

Rose just ran about getting in everyone's way. He seemed ever so excited.

'If he did have powers,' Piper said, as he raced past, 'you'd think this would have been his plan all along. Do you think he is lucky, Ollie? At all?'

I watched as Rose rolled around in Mum's basil. 'I'm finding it hard,' I admitted. Grandma seemed convinced that Rose was going to help, but I wasn't so sure.

'Oi, you two,' Grandma shouted down the garden. 'I'm doing everything here. Ollie?' She pointed to the house. 'Get some bedding. We need to line the basket. I wouldn't want Rose to fall through the damaged bit. How about that nice duvet of your mum's?'

I went inside and gathered up a heap of bedding and brought it out. Then I went back in for the leftover pizza and fizzy pop. It was a good thing we'd bought so much. There was enough to last for days.

I threw everything into the basket and climbed in after it. Once I'd stuffed the hole in the bottom with a sheet and spread Mum's duvet over the top, I leant back and watched the balloon billowing above. **Wow. Just look at it. It was huge.**

'What are you doing, Ollie?' Grandma peered over the edge. 'It's not nap time. We're almost ready to go. Here. Take Rose, will you?' She passed him down. 'Right. Mind out the way, I'm coming in.'

Piper scrambled after her. 'Isn't this brilliant, Ollie?' she said. 'Especially as we should be in **double maths**.'

It was brilliant. I'd watched Grandma take off loads of times, but I'd never been allowed to go with her.

'Hold tight!' Grandma tugged the handle that fired the burner.

WHOOOSH. The balloon started to rise. **OMG!** This was so much fun! I could see Mrs Frost from next door staring at us. I gave her a wave. We were off!

Oh. No. We weren't. The balloon came to a stop at roof height.

'Tut,' Grandma said. 'Ollie. It looks like you forgot to untie the anchor ropes.'

135

Me? I looked at her indignantly. No one had told me to untie the anchor ropes! How was I supposed to know?

'You'll have to pop back down.'

Eh? Was she kidding? I stood on a stack of pizza boxes and peered over the edge of the basket. We couldn't be that high, so why did it look so far to the ground? The rope ladder was swinging back and forth in the breeze. I checked to see if Piper wanted to do it instead, but she didn't.

'I'm looking after Rose,' she said. 'He's nervous. I don't think he likes heights.'

I didn't like heights either, but I wasn't going to say. Not in front of Piper. I pulled myself up on to the edge of the basket and turned around, and then I felt for the first rung with my foot. **Blimey**. It wasn't half swaying. I didn't dare look down. I held on as tight as I could and cautiously worked my way towards the bottom.

'Keep hold of the ladder, Ollie,' Grandma called

from above, 'or you'll be left behind.'

Well, that would be fantastic, wouldn't it? Stuck in Great Potton while Piper and Grandma went off to rescue Dad.

I did as Grandma said and hung on to the bottom rung as I untied the first three ropes. Then I got to the one I'd retied. I'd done such a good job, it wouldn't undo. Bum.

'Hurry up,' Piper called from above. Honestly! She was so annoying. I was doing my best!

I tugged on the wooden peg, but that wouldn't budge. I tried the knot again. **Blimey**. At this rate, I'd have to bite through it. Maybe I should go and get Myrtle? She'd make short work of it with her sharp hamster tee—

OMG!

MYRTLE!!!!

I'd forgotten about Myrtle!! I'd been so busy packing the basket I hadn't thought about Myrtle once. I was horrified with myself. I let go of the ladder and ran inside.

'Where are you going?' Grandma bellowed.

'Two secs,' I shouted back. Usually, if we go away, I take Myrtle round to Mrs Frost. I'd quickly do that, and then I'd get some scissors to cut through the— Eh? I looked around the kitchen. That was weird. Where was Myrtle's cage? Maybe Grandma had taken her next door already? I'd go and check. I ran down the hallway and flung open the front door.

Oh no!

There, on the step, were Bert and Ed.

22

I turned and ran full pelt back to the garden. I leapt on to the ladder and started to climb. **'Go, Grandma!'** I shouted. **'Quick! GO!'**

'What's going—' Grandma's face appeared over the edge of the basket. 'Oh. I see,' she said.

'Hold on tight, Ollie,' Piper shouted. There was a huge whoosh and the balloon shot upwards, pulling the final rope taut. The basket tilted and the ladder started to swing. For a moment, I thought I was going to fall off but I didn't. I focused on the basket and kept climbing.

'We just want to ask you about our dog,' shouted Ed, from below.

'What dog?' said Grandma. 'There's no dog here.'

'Rubbish.' Bert sounded pretty cross. **'We know you've got him.'**

I reached the top of the ladder and hauled myself into the basket. Phew.

'What on earth were you doing?' Grandma asked.

'Myrtle,' I croaked. 'I forgot to take her next door, and then I accidentally let them in.'

'Myrtle's in the rucksack,' Piper said. 'I didn't think we should leave her on her own.'

'You could have told me.' I scowled at her. 'I was really worried.'

'Sorry,' Piper said. 'Shall I get her out?'

I looked at Rose. Rose salivated. 'No,' I said. 'Better not.'

'Oi,' shouted Bert, from below.

Grandma pulled the burner handle again. The basket gave a lurch. She peered over the side. 'The peg's almost out,' she said. 'Once more should do it.'

'We only want to chat,' Bert called.

'Five minutes,' shouted Ed. 'Five minutes of your time in return for this "Make Your Own Sandwich" kit?' He held up two bits of bread.

'Sorry, we're in a rush,' said Grandma.

There was one last **WHOOSH**. The peg flew out of the ground and the balloon shot upwards. 'Au revoir, boys!' she shouted. 'Au revoir!'

We were off! I caught my breath as the balloon rose, higher and higher. This was amazing! It was ever so quiet. Grandma was looking at a map and Rose was in the corner, snoring gently. I stood on the pile of pizza boxes to get a better view. Piper climbed up beside me.

'Wow,' she said. 'I can see Tesco. And look at the school. It's tiny.'

'It must be break time.' I said. I was sure that was Thea Harris down there. I could see the sun glinting off her hair. I was disappointed she hadn't dropped a 'get well' card in. Maybe I should have given her protractor back?

We spent ages pointing out places we recognised until we were so high most things were just tiny little specks.

141

'Ollie?'

'What?' I said.

'If we're just going up, how do we actually get to Australia? '

'We find some air blowing in the right direction.' I said. It felt great knowing something that Piper didn't. 'It carries the balloon along.'

'For ten thousand miles?' Piper looked a bit doubtful. 'Won't that take ages?

Piper had a point. I mean, it was fun in the balloon, but it was ever so slow. 'Maybe,' I said, 'the higher we get, the faster the wind will be?'

Grandma glanced up from her map. 'Don't be so silly, Ollie.' She pointed towards the floor. 'I'm about to start the engine.'

Eh? Engine? What engine? 'Balloons don't have engines.' I said.

'This one does. How else do you think I won that race?'

My mouth dropped open. 'The Round the World in

Eighty Days Golden Jubilee Challenge? **You cheated?**'

Grandma looked outraged. 'How can you say such a thing, Ollie? You know me, I would **never** cheat. What a suggestion! My balloon was technically superior, that's all.' She rolled back the duvet and pulled open a small hatch. 'Now. Do you want to see this or not?'

I couldn't believe she'd cheated. She'd had her picture in the paper, and everything. Oh well – never mind. We had an engine! I leant forward for a better look.

'Your dad built this for his plane. It was an early version.' Grandma showed off a tangle of wires and tubes. 'He complained it wasn't powerful enough, so I borrowed it. He didn't mind. Well, he never said he minded, anyway, when he was looking all over the place for it, so he couldn't have done.'

'How does it work?' I asked.

'There's a solar panel sewn into the balloon. That powers most of it. The engine sucks in air and fires

143

it out of here.' She pointed at a shiny pipe. 'From the outside it looks just like a regular hot-air balloon. But it's not! It's got a jet-propelled basket. And over here ...' Grandma reached for a second hatch in the wall of the basket. She gestured proudly. 'A built-in satnav! I've already programmed it for Humpty Doo.'

'**Wow,**' said Piper. 'That's **incredible**.'

'Is it safe?' I asked. I nudged Rose awake with my foot, just in case we needed his lucky aura. 'Ollie. You know me. I would never take unnecessary risks. Ready?' She brandished a bottle. 'I tip distilled peanut oil into this funnel here ... see ... then I turn this dial ... set this gauge ... and press this switch.'

'Yikes,' shrieked Piper, as the balloon jolted. She fell off the pizza boxes. 'Is it supposed to do that?'

I clung on to Grandma. WOWEE! We were tearing through the air! The wind took my breath away. I ducked right down into the basket, where it was more sheltered. 'How fast are we going?' I shouted above the noise.

'No idea.' Grandma gave the engine a thump. 'It's stuck on full speed. Maybe a rhino sat on it?' She twiddled another dial. 'Oh well, better jammed on fast than slow.' She held a finger in the air. 'And the wind's behind us. At this rate, we'll be there by Thursday!'

23

Grandma had been over-optimistic. We weren't going to be there by Thursday. When we looked at the satnav, it said we'd we there on Friday, at 09:03.

'We've got ages,' Piper said. 'What shall we do, Ollie? It's too windy to look over the edge. Shall we play cards?'

I didn't like playing cards. I always lost. 'We didn't bring any,' I said.

'Yes, we did.' Grandma reached into her pocket. 'Can I play?'

'No. You always cheat,' I said.

'Rubbish, Ollie,' Grandma said. 'I'm just very good at cards, and you are not.'

Piper giggled. 'Once, at school,' she said, 'Ollie shouted "snap" every time he put a card down.'

'So?' said Grandma.

Piper smirked. 'We were playing poker.'

I glared at her. 'Let's play Old Maid,' I said. Are you going to deal, or shall I?'

Piper dealt. I looked at my cards. They were rubbish. I bet she'd fiddled them. Then I noticed Rose, snoozing in the corner. **Ah ha!** This could be my chance! If Rose really was lucky, perhaps I could harness his powers?

I waited till Grandma and Piper were looking the other way. Then I tempted him over with a doggie treat.

That should do it.

We played twelve games. Piper won every single one.

'So much for Rose,' I said. 'He isn't lucky at all.'

'He might be,' Piper said. 'I saw you give him that treat, so when you weren't looking, I gave him three.'

Grandma looked annoyed. 'In that case, Piper, Ollie and I win by default. You had an unfair advantage.'

'Or, possibly, said Piper, 'I'm just better at cards than both of you. Is it lunchtime yet?'

By Friday morning the air felt warmer – loads warmer. I crawled out of my sleeping bag and climbed on to the pizza boxes. **Wow!** Look at that beach! It was even better than Clacton! (Though, come to think of it, I couldn't see a pier, or any amusements, so maybe not.) Still, it was a shame we didn't have time to stop. 'Grandma,' I shouted. 'I think we're here!'

Grandma untangled herself from her duvet and came over. She peered down at the coast below. 'Fantastic,' she said. 'I told you that engine of your dad's was top notch. No wonder he spent so long looking for it.'

'Are we over Darwin?' Piper picked up Rose and climbed up to join us. 'Where are the swamps?'

'Everywhere,' said Grandma. 'The Northern Territory is massive. Hundreds of acres. What a place for your dad to crash! If it hadn't been for the lovely Bruce getting in touch, we'd have had no idea where to start looking.'

'How long till we land?' I asked.

'I've turned off the burner and cut the engine,' Grandma said. 'We're losing height already. Bruce is meeting us at the airfield. He's bringing a reporter from the local paper. *The Humpty Doo Herald*, I think.'

'What's he bringing a reporter for?' I asked.

'Publicity, Ollie. If everyone knows your dad's missing, then they'll keep an eye out. Bruce was keen for us to do an interview.'

Oh, OK. That seemed to make sense. I hoped the interview wouldn't take long, though. I wanted to get straight out there and start looking.

'Is Mum coming to meet us?' I asked.

'Oh no,' Grandma said. 'Definitely not. I asked Bruce not to say we were coming. I thought it would be much nicer to surprise her. We can catch up with her at the hotel.'

'Oh, OK,' I said.

'And I'd be grateful if you didn't mention the biscuits, or the gambling – or my balloon. And don't tell her about Rose either – she's a bit funny about animals.'

'No problem,' I said.

'She'll be absolutely thrilled to see you.'

I wasn't sure she would be. I was supposed to be studying.

I looked back over the edge. The beach was long gone, and all I could see below were trees. Acres and acres of them, dark green and squishy.

'According to the satnav –' Grandma tapped it – 'we're almost there. Why don't you unblock the hole in the floor, Ollie? Keep an eye out. You never know, you might spot your dad.'

Well, I didn't think that was very likely, as we were still really high, but I knelt down and pulled the sheet out of the hole anyway. It was a long, long way down. Miles. The rope ladder was swinging beneath the basket and ... **OMG!!!!**

Bert and Ed were on it!!!!

24

There they were. The two of them. Tied firmly to the ladder with Ed's hideous mustard scarf. I sat back in horror. They must have hopped on as we took off. I couldn't believe it. We'd brought them with us.

'Seen anything exciting?' Grandma said. 'A plane nose down in a swamp, for example?'

I shook my head.

'Are you OK, Ollie?' Piper asked. 'You look a bit weird.'

'It's Bert and Ed,' I said. 'They're on the ladder.'

'Bert and Ed?' Piper clutched Rose tighter. 'They're here?'

'Really?' Grandma peered through the hole.
'How rude.

They never asked if they could come along.'

'Oi, dog-lady? Is that you?' Bert looked furious.

'No,' Grandma called down. 'Definitely not.'

Piper giggled.

'Where exactly are we?' shouted Ed.

'*Australia.*'

Ed's face fell. 'But that's **miles**. I mean, I've always wanted to travel, but I've got the dentist this afternoon. Great Potton High Street. We'll never get back in time!'

'Never mind the dentist,' Bert's voice drifted up. 'Where's our dog?'

'I can't hear you,' Grandma said. 'It's blowy.'

'OUR DOG?' Bert shouted. 'WHERE IS IT?'

'I don't know about your dog,' said Grandma. 'Mine is just here.' She held Rose up. Rose gave a little yap.

'That's it. I'm coming up,' Bert said. He started to untie himself.

'Pardon?' said Grandma, cupping her ear.

'I'M COMING UP.'

152

'I'm afraid there's no room,' Grandma said. 'How about we go lower, and you hop off?'

'We're not hopping off anywhere without our dog.'

'Right.' Grandma pulled a penknife out of her bag and handed it over. 'Cut through the rope, Ollie.'

'Eh?' I said. 'But we're still really high.'

'Don't worry – I'll hover over a swamp. They'll have a soft landing. Come on. Get on with it.'

I climbed back on to the pizza boxes and reached for the rope attached to the ladder. Grandma's penknife looked ever so blunt. This was going to take a while. I began to saw.

'Oi!' Ed sounded a bit panicky as the ladder started to swing. **'Stop that!'**

'Just you wait,' shouted Bert. I looked over the edge. I could see his shiny bald head. He was getting closer.

'Piper?' I yelled. 'I need your help. See if you can find anything sharp.'

'Here you go.' Piper pulled Myrtle out of the

153

rucksack. 'Get her to use her teeth.'

Hamsters shouldn't be relied upon in tricky situations. Myrtle didn't help at all – she just ran around the edge of the basket. **Useless!** I sawed faster. I could do this. I had to do this. I was almost through! I glanced down. 'There's a swamp, Grandma!' I pointed. 'Fly over that.'

'Quick,' Piper said. 'Bert's nearly here.' She leant over the side and hurled a bit of pizza at him.

'I hope that's not the cheese and tomato, Piper?' Grandma looked up from the engine.

I frantically hacked at the last few strands. Nearly ... nearly ... nearly ... Yes! The basket swung violently. I clutched at the side but missed and toppled down on to Grandma. Rose almost fell through the hole, but Piper grabbed her just in time.

'There they go.' Piper peered through the bottom of the basket. 'My, what a splash!'

'Are they OK?' I said.

'They're fine – look.'

Bert and Ed were floundering about in the mud below. They shouted something up at us.

'Rude.' Grandma tutted. 'Don't repeat that, Ollie, will you? Not in front of your mum, anyway.'

'I'm not surprised they're cross. Shall we give them a map?'

'Good idea,' said Piper. She threw one down. 'They can have the rest of the pepperoni as well. No one likes that.'

Grandma stood up and brushed herself down. 'What were they thinking, hitching a ride? The cheek of it! Piper, stuff that hole back up, would you, we almost lost Rose. What a lucky escape!'

'Hang on.' Piper went pale.

'What?' I said.

'Where's Myrtle?'

'Myrtle?'

MYRTLE!!!

I looked up at the edge of the basket but I couldn't see her. Then I looked under all the duvets. She wasn't there. There weren't many places to look in a balloon basket, but I looked everywhere, including in Rose's mouth. Twice.

She must have fallen off when the balloon jolted. I stood there, trying not to cry. Not Myrtle.

'She must be here,' said Piper. She lifted up some pizza boxes. **'She must be.'**

But she wasn't.

Myrtle had gone.

'What do you want to do, Ollie?' Grandma asked. 'I can set the basket down. We might be able to find her.'

'I'm sorry.' Piper was properly crying. 'I was only trying to help.'

'It's not your fault.' I found it hard to say that, and I only said it because I could see Piper was feeling terrible. I mean, it WAS her fault. She'd brought Myrtle with us. SHE had put her on the edge of the basket. Of COURSE it was her fault. I'd never seen her cry before, though.

Even Rose looked sad, but that was probably because he'd missed out on a furry snack.

I looked over the edge of the basket at all the trees. They stretched for miles. It was going to be hard enough to find Dad out there, let alone a tiny hamster.

'Ollie?'

'We need to keep going,' I said. My heart broke a little bit.

'Are you sure?' Grandma asked. She patted me on the shoulder.

'Yep,' I said. 'I'm sure. Dad's more important.'

He was, but I still felt awful.

Poor Myrtle. I was really, **really** going to miss her.

25

'**The airfield is** a couple of miles to our right,' said Grandma, tapping the satnav. 'We'll be landing shortly.'

The trees had thinned out, and we'd started to see tracks and farm buildings. Now, beneath us, was the tiny town of Humpty Doo.

'There's not much there,' Piper said.

There wasn't. There was a crossroads and a few houses and something that looked like a petrol station. There was one bigger building with a corrugated roof, which Grandma said was Bruce's hotel.

'Where's the pool?' said Piper. 'Is it an indoor one? Maybe it's in that building behind? That one there. The wooden one.'

'What makes you think there's a pool?' I said.

'Of course there is. It's a hotel! It's bound to have a pool.'

Grandma brought the balloon down with the smallest of bumps. She's ever so good at ballooning when she wears her glasses. And until Myrtle fell out – poor Myrtle – it had been a brilliant flight.

I couldn't wait. I leapt out of the basket. We were here! WOW. Just look at it. Australia seemed to go on for ever. There were acres of yellow grass, and far in the distance, a dark green wall of trees.

It was ever so hot. **Ridiculously hot.**

It was nothing like Great Potton. It was very dusty. And pretty empty. I could only see one building, right at the end of the airstrip. Was that the airfield terminal? It wasn't very big. Eh? I squinted through the haze. Were its doors opening? Yes. They were.

A crowd of people spilled out on to the tarmac. They paused for a moment, then I saw someone point in our direction. Eh? Were they all heading this way? I took a step backwards.

Piper appeared beside me. 'I'd better find the sun cream,' she said. 'Gingers don't do well in the hea—Oh.' She stared at the throng charging towards us. 'Who are they? Why have they all got cameras?

'I think they're reporters.'

'What are they taking pictures of?' She glanced over her shoulder. 'We're the only ones here.'

I took another step back. This was weird. Hot, sandy and weird.

Grandma bustled up with Rose in her arms. 'Oooh, look,' she said. 'How lovely. A welcome party!' She shielded her eyes from the sun. 'Gracious! That must be Bruce.'

In front of the pack galloped a man with a bright red face and slicked-back hair. His moustache was suspiciously black. He was wearing a tight safari jacket and very short shorts.

'Ms Brown?' The man leading the way screeched to a halt in front of Grandma. He held out a chubby hand. 'So pleased to meet you! Is this your balloon?' He took a step back and gazed up at it. 'What an **enchanting** mode of transport. Do let me introduce myself.' He bowed. 'Bruce. Mr Bruce Loops.'

Grandma shook his hand to an explosion of flashes. 'A pleasure, Mr Loops,' she said, blinking.

'No need to be formal.' He gave a little chortle. 'Call me Bruce. Actually, some friends call me Loopy Bruce; I've no idea why. **I'm not loopy at all!'**

'Bruce. You may call me Florence.' Grandma smiled graciously and gave a little curtsy. Eh? Who did she think she was? The Queen?

Bruce bent low over her hand. 'Florence,' he said. 'Charmed.'

'Is she blushing?' whispered Piper.

Bruce gave Grandma's hand one last squeeze before dropping it and turning to me.

'Ollie?'

He patted me on the head! Eh? How old did he think I was? Three?

'Such a terrible shame, Ollie. Both your parents going missing.' He beckoned across a reporter carrying a microphone. 'How do you feel about that?'

Both my parents missing? I stared at him. 'Eh?' I said.

The reporter pointed his microphone at my face.

Bruce nodded. 'I'm afraid, Ollie, **your mother's missing too.'** He looked mournfully into the TV camera. 'She arrived yesterday and went straight out to search for your dad. We haven't heard from her since. We were wondering if a dingo got her.'

'Oh, I wouldn't worry about Sukey, Bruce,' Grandma said. 'She's very capable. Annoyingly capable if you ask me. She'll turn up.'

'I gave her a map,' Bruce said. 'Couldn't stop her. Very stubborn lady.'

'Maybe you should have gone with her,' I said. 'Seeing as you invited her.'

He gave a little giggle. 'Gracious, Ollie, that would have been impossible! My hotel won't run itself, and I have all these fine gentlemen to look after.' He glanced over at the reporters and raised his voice. 'That's Humpty Doo Towers, by the way. Don't forget to mention that, ladies and gents of the press.'

He turned back to me. 'And your dad? What do you think, Ollie? What got him? **A croc?'**

'We don't know anything got him yet,' I said. 'Actually.'

Bruce turned to the crowd behind him. 'The boy's weeping. You could get a good shot here.'

Weeping? **I wasn't weeping!!** I pushed the TV camera away from my face.

Piper giggled. 'Would you like a tissue, Ollie?' she said.

'Absolutely not, thanks, Piper.'

Bruce patted my shoulder. 'It's fine, Ollie, fine. Let it all out. You're among friends.'

What a twit.

Bruce suddenly spotted Rose. 'What a splendid little woofer! Is he yours, Florence?'

'He certainly is.' Grandma held Rose out to be admired. 'I've not had him long,' she said. 'He's adorable, isn't he?'

'Like his owner.' Bruce gave Grandma a wink.

'**<u>GROSS,</u>**' Piper muttered.

I glared at Bruce. Grandma seemed to like him. I didn't. I couldn't believe he'd let Mum go off on her own.

'Grandma?' I said. 'Shall I get our rucksacks?

'Sorry, Ollie?' Grandma blinked. 'Oh yes. Of course. The rucksacks. Good idea.'

'I have a truck. The kids can load it up.' Bruce turned to the journalists. 'You can ask your questions back at the hotel.' He struck a pose.

'That's Humpty Doo Towers, for your notebooks – the finest hotel in town.'

'The only hotel, as far as I can see,' Piper said.

26

Humpty Doo Towers didn't actually have any towers. It was built out of breeze blocks and stuck all over with adverts for beer and frankfurters. Inside it was dark, and smelt of old vegetables. Piper looked disappointed. 'My expectations have not been met,' she whispered. 'I thought hotels were classy?'

'Your room's this way. Come along.' Bruce trotted down a corridor ahead of us. 'Don't mind the cobwebs.'

'Can't see them for the dust,' said Piper.

'Loo's on the left. Always check for **REDBACKS**,' said Bruce, over his shoulder. 'You don't want a nasty nip on the **clacker**.'

'I know a redback's a spider, but what's a clacker?' Piper said, racing to keep up.

'Never mind,' I said.

'And here you are!' Bruce flung open a door. 'You're OK sharing, aren't you?'

'Oh,' I said.

'Nice,' said Piper.

Considering Bruce had used words like 'lap of luxury' and 'splendid', the room was smaller than I'd expected, and quite grubby. There were three narrow bunks on one wall, with just enough room to squeeze in alongside.

Grandma didn't seem to mind. She threw her stuff on to the top bunk and went off with Bruce to be shown around.

Piper shuffled sideways to the window at the end and looked out.

'I never realised Australia was so big,' she said. 'There's an awful lot of it.'

It was big. **Big – and full of spiders and snakes and dingoes.** Poor Dad. Poor Mum. How on earth were we going to find them?

Grandma stuck her head back in. Rose was draped

around her shoulders like a cape. 'Ollie? Bruce wants to know if you're ready to do the press conference.'

'Come on, Piper,' I said. I didn't feel like facing the reporters on my own.

Grandma coughed delicately. 'I think he just wants you, Ollie. They're **your** parents, after all.'

Oh. I looked at Piper to see if she minded.

'Don't worry,' said Piper. 'I'm used to it. No one ever wants me.'

'It's not personal,' Grandma said.

'It never is,' Piper said. She sat down on the bunk. 'I'll just wait here, shall I, out of sight?'

'You're welcome to come and watch. Bruce won't mind that. He's such a lovely man. And so generous! He just said that anyone who comes to help can stay at reduced rates!'

'Well, I hope they have better rooms than ours.' Piper muttered. 'And the reporters are probably hoping we'll be eaten by alligators. Think of the headlines!'

Bruce was waiting for me in the hotel restaurant. He'd pushed a long dining table to the end of the room and was lounging behind it. The reporters were sitting around in small groups, looking a bit bored.

A couple of flashes went off as I came in.

'Where's the dog?' Bruce clicked his fingers. 'Florence? Let him hold the dog. The public love a picture of a dog.'

'On my way, Bruce.' Grandma rushed over, unwinding Rose from her neck. She plopped him on my lap. 'Here you go, Ollie.'

Rose buried his nose in his paws. He looked hot and tired and fed up. I felt sorry for him. I didn't want to be here either, having to answer stupid questions. I wanted to be out in the bush,

looking for Mum and Dad.

When I looked up, the reporters were all staring at me. I gulped. **The TV camera was pointing straight towards my face.** They were waiting for me to say something! I opened my mouth and then shut it again. I looked at Bruce and shook my head. I wasn't good at this sort of thing at all!

Bruce leant over. 'Come on,' he muttered in my ear. 'This is your moment. Talk about your dad.' He picked up a little mallet and hammered the table.

'Um ...' I said.

Grandma waved encouragingly. 'Go on,' she said. 'Tell them about the plane.'

I took a deep breath. I didn't look at the reporters, I looked straight ahead. 'My dad built an aeroplane,' I said. 'Only a small one. The engine ran on peanut oil. He wanted to show you could fly around the world on a single tank of fuel.'

Someone tittered. Well, that was nice! I ignored them and carried on. 'Anyway. He crashed. Now he's missing. He's been missing for weeks. We don't know why, he's a really good explorer. We've come to try and find him.'

'And that thing on your lap? Did you bring it to help? Is it some kind of bloodhound?' There were a few more sniggers from the back.

'Actually,' I said, 'he's an **Ancient Dog of Destiny.** A teller of fortune and bringer of luck. We're ...' My voice petered out. Grandma was shaking her head violently, and dragging her finger across her throat.

It looked like she didn't want me to talk about Rose.

'Ha ha,' I said. 'Only joking. He's a completely regular dog.'

Bruce elbowed me. 'Move on,' he muttered. 'They're not really interested in your gran's scruffy little mutt.'

He'd changed his tune! I thought he liked Rose!

I started again. 'Dad—'

'How are you finding the hotel?' Bruce interrupted.

Eh? What sort of question was that? 'Um ... it's fine, I suppose,' I said.

'Hear that?' Bruce gesticulated wildly. 'Fine. A FINE establishment, he says. Humpty Doo Towers! Fit for a king!'

I stood up. I'd had enough. 'It was really nice of you all to come,' I said, politely, 'but I need to go and find my dad now.'

Bruce leant over and leered into the TV camera. 'Make a weekend break of it,' he said. 'Humpty Doo Towers. Bring the kids. Bring your nan! Let's all help Ollie find his father!'

He was making it sound like it was some kind of game show! 'Come on, Rose,' I said. 'Let's go.' I pushed my chair aside and started to walk out.

'Wait!' Bruce came galloping after me.

Rose scrabbled in my arms. He probably wanted to nip Bruce's fat ankles. 'What?'

'Where's your friend?' he asked. 'That girl?'

I shrugged. 'In our room, I think.'

'I forgot to warn you.' Bruce looked serious.

'About what?'

'The yard. Don't go out there.'

'Why not?'

'There's a nest of **rattlers**. Evil creatures. One bite is all it takes. I need to deal with them. Haven't got around to it yet. Busy busy. Make sure you tell your friend, won't you?'

'OK.' I kept walking. 'I'll tell her.'

'Make sure you do,' he called after me.

27

'**Bruce is nuts,**' I said to Gran.

'He's a little *flamboyant*, perhaps?' Grandma pulled down her rucksack from the top bunk. 'But charming, all the same.'

'He's a fame hound,' Piper walked in behind us. 'I saw him, posing for the camera.'

'Where have you been?' I asked.

'I went to look for the swimming pool,'

'I hope you didn't go out the back?' I said. 'You're not supposed to. There are snakes.'

'I didn't see any.' Piper held her arms out for Rose. 'There wasn't a pool either. Unless it was in the outbuilding – and that was locked.'

'Wait up, folks!' Bruce stuck his head round the door and then squeezed himself into the room. Rose yapped. He really didn't like Bruce.

'Are you coming with us?' I said. I didn't want him to, but I supposed the more people out there looking, the better.

'Gracious, no,' Bruce said. 'Far too busy. **Far, FAR too busy.** I'll mark your map up though.'

He grabbed it from under Grandma's arm and held it

flat against the wall. 'We're here.' He tapped the middle of the map with a stubby finger. 'And this –' he pointed to another area – 'is where I was when the plane flew over. Just here, by this **swamp**.'

'That's not far at all!' Grandma peered closely. 'Five miles – if that.

In fact, I'd say it's just about where we dropped Bert and Ed off.'

Well, that was good. Crocs weren't all we'd have to watch out for.

Bruce ignored her and went on. 'I heard a thud a minute or so later.' He pulled a pencil from behind his ear and brandished it. 'I therefore believe, Ollie, your dad crashed just about ... um ...' He thought about it. **'Here.'** He finally scribbled a cross two inches to the right of the swamp.

'I can't believe he didn't make it to Humpty Doo,' I said. 'He must have set off in completely the wrong direction.'

Piper gave Bruce a pointed look. 'It's a shame you didn't think to go and investigate at the time,' she said.

'I'm a busy man,' Bruce said. 'I had to get the snags on for breakfast.'

'Of course you did.' Grandma folded the map and popped it in her bag. 'Snags are sausages, Piper. Thank you, Bruce. You've been extremely helpful.'

'Yeah, thanks,' I muttered. I didn't mean it. In fact,

once Grandma and Bruce were out of earshot, I made it quite clear to Piper I hadn't meant it at all.

'He's **horrible**,' I said. 'Leaving Dad out there like that. I don't understand him at all. All he seems to care about is getting his face on the telly.'

'He was on TV, once,' Piper said. 'There's a clipping up in the loo. It was a show called *Bush Oyster Buffet*. He won some money and bought this hotel.'

'I know,' I said. 'I heard him telling Grandma. Several times.'

'No one ever comes to stay,' Piper said. 'It's about to go bust.'

'How do you know that?' I said.

'There was a letter on the side. From the bank.'

Honestly! Piper was so nosy! 'You're not supposed to read other people's mail,' I said.

Piper shrugged. 'It was just there,' she said. 'It wasn't in an envelope or anything. **I was bored.**'

'Even so,' I said.

'Oh, stop being such a **goody-goody**, Ollie. I

thought it was interesting, that's all.

'Why?' I said.

'Well, the hotel's full now, isn't it?'

'What's that got to do with anything?'

She looked at me. 'I don't think Bruce cares about finding your dad. He's using what happened to get publicity for the hotel.'

I looked at her. From what I'd seen of Bruce, she was probably right.

28

I went inside to find Grandma. I wanted to get going. She was in our room, shoving things into rucksacks.

'Ollie. You take this one.' She handed it into the corridor. 'It's got the cooking equipment in it. Piper's is over there. She's carrying the waterproofs.'

Blimey. Mine was heavy. When Grandma turned her back I took a frying pan out and stuffed it into Piper's. Perhaps I could pop something in Grandma's too. 'Where's yours?' I asked.

She held up her handbag.

'Is that it?'

'I'm not sure what you are implying, Ollie. This bag is extremely weighty. I not only have the map and compass – two items crucial to the success of our trip – but I will be in charge of Rose, an elderly dog, who will need careful supervision at all times.'

Rose was looking sprightly, if you asked me. He was jumping up at the window, snapping at flies.

'Who's got the food?' I asked.

'We don't need any. I shall be teaching you the ways of the wild. There will be all sorts of **delicious** things we can snack on.'

'Like what?'

Grandma ignored me. She scooped Rose up off the windowsill and tied a string on to his collar. 'Now,' she said, 'what else? Ah, Piper, there you are. This is your last chance to use the loo, if you need to go?'

'I'm fine. Is that one mine?' Piper picked up her rucksack. She didn't even mention the weight of it, which was surprising. She'd start complaining soon, though. She didn't have explorer genes, like me.

'I've given Bruce our ETR,' Grandma said, as we walked down the corridor.

'What's ETR?'

I was glad Piper asked, as I had no idea.

'Estimated Time of Return,' Grandma held the

180

door. 'In case we get delayed, and he has to send out a search party.'

'Can't you just text him?' I said. I shielded my eyes from the sun. Wow, it was hot out here. Boiling.

'The phone signal is terrible in Humpty Doo, Ollie. Very erratic. Your dad was lucky to find one when he made that call home.'

'He was up a tree,' I said. 'Maybe that helped?'

'Maybe.' She popped Rose down on the ground. 'Walkies, Rose. **Walkies**.'

'Have you got the map?' I asked.

'We don't need it, Ollie. This is Rose's chance to shine. He can lead the way.'

Fantastic! We waited eagerly.

Rose sat down. He sat down and he looked at us and then he put his head down on his paws and closed his eyes.

'He's thinking,' Grandma murmured, reverently.

'Come on, Rose,' I said. 'Get up.'

'Don't hurry him,' hissed Grandma. 'This is

important. He needs time.'

Rose gave a gentle snore.

'Shall we just use the map?' said Piper.

I prodded Rose with my toe. Only gently, but it did the trick. Rose opened his eyes and got slowly to his feet.

'Marvellous,' said Grandma. She grabbed his lead. **'We're off.'**

We weren't. Not really. Rose meandered one way, and then the other, and then he went and scratched at the hotel door. Then he sat down again and yawned.

I crouched next to him. 'Please, Rose?' I said. 'Even if you're not lucky, can't you just use your nose? *Even regular dogs can follow a scent.'*

Rose gazed at the trees in the distance. He sniffed the air and snapped at a fly. Then he stood up. Was he going to go? Yay! He was!

'He's on to something,' Grandma shouted. 'Keep up or we'll lose him.'

Rose sped across the scrub and we followed

behind as close as we could. Oh, my, it was hot. I was puffing and panting and dripping in seconds. The rucksack straps were digging into my shoulders and the only thing I could think about was how much I needed a drink.

'How much further?' I asked.

'Miles, I should think,' said Grandma, **'considering we only just left.'**

I gritted my teeth. Rose was bounding ahead, as fresh as a daisy. He looked like he knew exactly where he was going. I hoped he did. Piper was charging along too. Her rucksack didn't seem to be bothering her at all. That was annoying, as it meant I couldn't complain about mine.

Once we got to the trees it wasn't as bad. It was still boiling but at least it was shady.

'Careful of the snakes,' Grandma said. 'They don't like being picked up. And most of the spiders are deadly, so no mucking about with them, either.'

I wasn't likely to do any 'mucking about' with

spiders. I stepped on a pointy twig. 'Ow,' I said.

'What's wrong?' Grandma asked.

'I'm fine,' I said. 'It's hard going though.'

'Really?' Grandma said. 'You need toughening up. How about a snack?'

That sounded good. Grandma had probably brought along some cereal bars or flapjacks. I dropped my rucksack and collapsed on the ground in a heap.

'Oh, come on, Ollie,' Piper said. 'You can't be that tired.'

I was. It was so hot I could hardly breathe and my shoulders were killing me. I couldn't believe Grandma and Dad did this sort of thing for fun. It was awfu— **OMG!** I was struck by a terrible thought.

Maybe I didn't have explorer genes after all????

Maybe they'd skipped me?

No. That couldn't be right. I just needed some practice.

'Here you go,' said Grandma. 'I was foraging as

we walked.' She dropped something into my hand. 'These should give you some energy.'

I looked up at her. Was she serious? **Maggots?**

'Share them with Piper, won't you?'

'I'm good, thank you,' Piper said. 'I'll just have a drink.'

'What are they?' I said, watching them squirm about.

'Witchetty grubs,' Grandma said. **'Little parcels of wormy goodness.'**

Whatever they were, they were fat and yellow and staring straight at me. *DID* explorers really eat grubs? Why? Why wouldn't they just bring sandwiches?

'They're nice, Ollie. A bit gristly – but full of flavour.' Grandma watched me expectantly.

I had to eat them. I had to prove myself. I did have explorer genes. I did.

'Watch out!' Piper jumped to her feet. 'A snake!'

Grandma grabbed Rose. She held him aloft. 'Where?'

I saw my chance. I hurled the grubs into a bush.

'There.'

Grandma peered in the direction Piper was pointing. 'I can't see anything. It must have slithered off. How are the grubs, Ollie?'

I chewed. 'Great,' I said. 'Really tasty. What's for pudding?

'If you're still hungry, you can pick berries as we walk. That's what I've been doing. Shall we get going?' Grandma brushed the front of her top. I looked at her suspiciously. Were those crumbs? Berries weren't very crumby. Where would crumbs come from?

I decided to find out. 'Shall I carry your bag for a bit?' I offered.

'That's kind, Ollie. I mean, my bag might not look heavy compared to all the stuff you two have got, but let me tell you – it jolly well is.' She handed it over.

I waited till she'd turned her back and then I opened it.

Her bag was stuffed with biscuit wrappers!

How could she? I'd almost eaten maggots, and all the while she'd been scoffing custard creams!

I'd had enough. I told Grandma what I thought of her behaviour and stormed ahead, thwacking at the undergrowth with a stick. I was the only one who seemed to be taking this trip seriously! Stupid Grandma. Stupid Piper. Stupid Rose, who was most definitely, and absolutely, not a Dog of Destiny, not a teller of fortune, or a bringer of luck.

I pushed my way through a thicket into a clearing.

Eh?

Well, that definitely wasn't lucky.

I'd run straight into Bert and Ed.

29

They were sitting on a log next to a swamp. If I hadn't been muttering to myself about the custard creams, I might have been able to creep away. As it was, I had no chance.

Ed swung round. **'HEY!'** he said. **'LOOK WHO IT IS.'**

I wasn't sure what to do. Should I run? Should I shout to warn Grandma and Piper? Should I attack?

I took a step backwards.

Bert got to his feet. 'It's Ollie, isn't it?'

I took another step back and tripped over a root.

Ed got up too. 'We only wanted our dog back.' He looked pretty annoyed. 'Now look. Here we are, totally lost and miles from home.'

'You can't blame me for being lost,' I said. 'We threw you a map.'

Bert looked around. 'Where is the little mutt anyway?'

I scrambled to my feet. 'Rose? You can't have him. If he is lucky, we need him.'

'Yeah well. I'm not sure he even is a blooming Dog of Destiny,' said Ed. He slapped at a mosquito. 'We've had nothing but trouble since we found him.'

'You can't say that,' said Bert. 'The old lady took him before we'd had a proper go.'

'We won some money,' I said. 'But we haven't found my dad yet.'

'Tell you what, I'll **swap** you,' Bert said.

'Swap me? Swap me for what?'

Bert reached inside his jacket and pulled out something small and fluffy. 'It fell out of the basket,' he said. 'I rescued it.'

MYRTLE!!!

I could have wept with joy. I'd felt so awful about abandoning her – and now here she was, alive and kicking! (Well, not kicking – hamsters don't really kick.)

'OK,' I said. 'I'll see. I can't promise anything

though. Grandma's really attached to Rose.'

'OK,' said Bert. 'You take this in the meantime. Horrid little ratty thing. I'm sure I'm allergic.'

'Thanks,' I said as he handed Myrtle over. **'Thanks so much.'**

As I took her, there was a rustling behind me. I swung around in case it was a croc sneaking up through the rushes, but it wasn't. It was Piper and Grandma.

'Oh no,' said Piper. 'It's the bad guys.'

'Eh,' said Bert. 'How come we're the bad guys? You stole our dog and dumped us in a swamp.'

He did have a point, I suppose.

'Are you all right, Ollie?' Grandma asked. 'What's that you've got?

'IT'S MYRTLE!' I held her out.

'OMG! THAT'S FANTASTIC,' said Piper.

'He swapped her for the dog,' Ed said.

'Pardon?' said Grandma. 'Did you say he swapped her?'

'Actually,' I said. 'I didn't. I said I'd see what I could do.'

'You can't swap something that doesn't belong to you, Ollie,' said Grandma piously.

'I think you'll find he doesn't belong to you either,' said Bert. **'DOG ROBBER.'**

'Where did you get him from, then?'

'Um ...' Bert looked a bit flustered. 'We, um, were just driving along, like, and we found him. Just by the side of ...'

'Oh, rubbish,' said Grandma. 'That was my story. Anyway. You can't have him. I'm very fond of him, lucky or not.'

'Where is he?' Ed looked around. 'I hope nothing's happened to him?'

'He ran off,' said Piper. 'We were going to go after him, but we thought we should find Ollie first.'

'So you've lost our dog?' said Ed.

'Oh, for the last time,' said Grandma, **'he's not yours.'**

'WE need him,' said Bert.

'So do **we,'** said Grandma.

'Not as much as **US,'** said Ed.

'YOU'RE just after money,' Piper said.

'RUBBISH,' Bert said. 'We're not interested in becoming extremely rich. Not at all. We're ... um ... um ... Scout leaders.'

Eh? Scout leaders? I gave them a suspicious look. 'I'm a Scout,' I said. 'How come I've never seen you?'

'We're based in Small Potton, not Great Potton,' Bert said quickly. 'So you won't recognise us. Anyway. We need to raise funds for our Scout hut. It's leaking. There's water all over the place. We can't do any ... um ... Scouting, until the roof is fixed. Some awful woman from Health and Safety said so.'

'That was probably your mum,' said Piper. I trod on her foot.

'We've got nowhere else to meet,' Bert went on. 'It's a crying shame. The children are devastated. We need ... um ...' He looked at Ed.

'Ten thousand pounds,' said Ed.

'That's right,' Bert said. 'At least ten thousand. I mean, we held a cake sale and a raffle – all legit, of course – but it wasn't enough.' He sighed loudly. 'We didn't know what to do. Then Ed read about the lucky dog on Wikipedia. So, we found out where he'd last been seen, and then, we, um, acquired him. **COMPLETELY HONESTLY,** like.'

'We were hoping he'd help us win something. You know, from a scratch card, or a lottery ticket.' Ed shook his head sadly. 'But then he was taken.' He gave Grandma a glare.

'Well, why didn't you say? If it's for the Scouts.' Grandma opened her bag. 'We've got **loads** left over from our winnings.' She took out a big wad of notes.

'Here you go. You have the money, and I'll keep Rose.'

'Seriously?' Bert looked delighted.

'Hang on,' said Piper. She looked a bit miffed. 'Shouldn't we keep some back for – I don't know – emergencies ... and pizzas?'

'Think of the Scouts,' said Bert. He snatched the cash from Grandma and tucked it into his pocket. 'Come on, Ed, let's go and, um, mend that roof.'

'There's easily enough for that – and your flights home,' Grandma called after them. 'Humpty Doo Airfield is that way. Best of luck.' She smiled warmly as they disappeared into the rushes. 'First impressions are never what they seem, are they, Ollie? I had them down as complete ruffians, but actually, they have hearts of gold.'

I wasn't so sure. They still seemed pretty dodgy to me.

'I can't believe you gave them all that cash,' Piper said. 'To keep a dog that doesn't seem very lucky.'

'Lucky or not,' Grandma said, 'I'm extremely fond

of Rose. I'd have paid **twice** as much.' She slung her handbag over her shoulder. 'Now. We need to find him. Piper. Did you see which way he went?'

'No idea,' said Piper. 'We'd better retrace our steps.'

'You two stick together,' Grandma said. 'Stay within shouting distance. I'll try this way.' She charged off through the undergrowth.

'How's Myrtle, Ollie?' Piper asked as we made our way back the way we'd come. 'Is she all right?'

'She's fine,' I said. 'I can't believe I got her back – hey! I can hear yapping!'

Piper pointed. 'Over there.'

Rose sounded frantic. I started to run. **I hoped he hadn't been bitten by a snake.** We'd only covered gnat bites at Scouts. I left the path and pushed my way into a clearing. Where was he?

There he was, jumping up and down at the foot of a eucalyptus tree, yapping and yapping and yapping. He must have chased a possum, or maybe a koala?

'Rose,' I shouted, picking up speed. 'Stop it.'

Rose took no notice and carried on bouncing. Piper came up behind me.

'What's he doing?'

'Being an idiot,' I said. What was he making such a fuss about? I leant against the trunk and peered into the lower branches. There was something up there, something swinging in the leaves. I craned my neck. Rose hurled himself against my legs, yapping frantically. 'Rose!' I said. 'Just stop it, will you?' I picked him up and tried to calm him down.

'Ollie?'

I looked over my shoulder at Piper. 'What?'

She looked puzzled. 'I didn't say anything,'

'You said my name.'

She shook her head. 'No, I didn't.'

'Someone did.' I looked around. 'Hello?'

A voice floated down from the branches. 'Ollie? Is that you? Be careful. That thing's ferocious!'

<u>OMG.</u> That sounded like ... I looked back up.

'Mum?'

30

She was dangling from above, tangled in some kind of netting.

'Blimey,' said Piper. 'That's a bit high for your mum.'

'Hang on,' Mum shouted down. 'I'm cutting myself free. I was **almost** out when that awful creature turned up. **Don't let him bite you.** Mind out the way.'

I stepped back as she swung down through the branches and landed in front of me. 'Ollie,' she said. 'Ollie.'

I gave her a massive hug.

'I'm so glad you're OK,' I said. 'Bruce thought a dingo had got you. I was a bit worried.'

'I'm fine.' Mum hugged me back. For ages. She looked a bit dazed. 'I left you in Great Potton with Grandma,' she said. 'What are you doing here? **You're supposed to be studying.'**

'We decided to come and help,' I said. 'And when we got here, Bruce said you'd gone off by yourself.'

Mum snorted. 'He was too busy talking to the press. I wasn't going to wait for him.'

'You don't normally do anything risky.' I said. 'It's not like you.'

'I was OK till that happened.' Mum scowled upwards. 'I mean, Bruce said there were crocodile traps, but he also said I'd be totally fine if I stuck to the path.'

Rose gave a little yip.

Mum looked at him doubtfully. 'What is that?' she asked. 'Some kind of bush rat? Careful, Ollie. Its teeth look ever so sharp.'

'Rose is a very rare Egyptian Choodle,' I said. 'He's Grandma's. He's amazing. He's lucky.'

'And he might look a bit scruffy,' said Piper, 'but he's very clean. We gave him a bath. Your shampoo smel— **OW!**'

I stepped off her foot. 'Mum,' I said. 'This is Piper. Remember? From school?'

'Hi, Ollie's mum,' Piper said. 'How's Aunt Lucy?'

Mum blushed. 'Yes, well,' she said. 'Sorry about that, but I didn't want Ollie to insist on coming.'

'Mum,' I said. 'You're going to have to stop fussing some time. **I'm eleven.'**

'I know,' she said. 'I'm sorry. I can't help it. I couldn't bear it if something happened to you.'

'Is that why you want Ollie to be an accountant?' asked Piper. 'So he's safe?'

Mum looked uncomfortable. 'I just want him to have **options**,' she said.

I thought back to the witchetty grubs and

shuddered. 'I wouldn't worry,' I said. 'I'm not sure I'm cut out to be an explorer.'

'He's right, actually,' Piper said. 'You should have heard him **whinging** about the heat and the flies, and having to carry stuff.'

'Shall we get on?' I said. 'We've wasted enough time chatting.'

'OK,' Piper said. 'Careful, though. I can hear something rustling.' She pointed at some reeds. 'Over there.'

Mum whipped a knitting needle out of her pocket and shoved me to one side. **'Stand back,'** she said. 'I'll deal with this.'

Blimey, I'd never seen Mum on the attack! She slashed the knitting needle through the air and stabbed at imaginary beasts. I had a nasty flashback to my dream and the exploding crocodile, so I was relieved when it was Grandma who burst out of the grass.

'Sukey! They found you!' She looked

thrilled. **'Fandabbytastic!** How are you finding the outback? Fun, isn't it?'

'Florence.' Mum didn't look very pleased, but she put her knitting needle away, which was a relief. 'I might have known. You said you'd keep Ollie out of trouble.'

'And I have!' Grandma waved towards me. 'Look at him. Not in trouble at all. A picture of health. Glowing, in fact.'

'That's sunburn,' said Mum. 'I guess you forgot to put any lotion on him?'

'We came to rescue you,' Grandma said. 'I thought you'd be pleased.'

'As you can see, I didn't need rescuing.' Mum sounded frosty. That wasn't good. I thought about the mess we'd left the kitchen in. And the casino. And all the other stuff. We should probably get going before Mum asked any more questions.

'Shall we start looking for Dad, then?' I said.

201

'Good idea,' Grandma said. 'I suppose you haven't found him?' She looked at Mum.

'No,' Mum said. She looked away. 'No, I haven't.'

'No sign at all?' Grandma pressed.

Mum's bottom lip started to quiver. 'Oh, Florence,' she said. She dropped her rucksack on to the ground and sat on it.

'Are you all right?' Piper asked.

Mum put her face in her hands.

We all stood and looked at her, waiting for her to say something.

Rose wandered over and flopped down next to her. She didn't push him away. She stroked him. Mum wouldn't normally do that. Not a germy old dog. Something must be really wrong.

'What?' I asked. 'What?'

She burst into tears.

'Tell us, Mum.' I said. I was finding it hard to breathe.

She looked up at me. 'We're too late.'

'What do you mean?' I sat down next to her and took her hand.

She looked at me and shook her head.

'OH, OLLIE. DAD'S BEEN EATEN.'

31

'**Don't be so** silly, Sukey.' Grandma crouched down. 'What on earth makes you think that?'

I'd never seen her look worried before. About anything.

Mum wiped her eyes. She reached for her rucksack and rummaged inside. 'Here,' she said. She held something out.

'What is it?' asked Piper.

'It's the hat I knitted for him before he left. In case it got cold at night.'

I could hardly bear to look at it, but I did. It was definitely Dad's hat. **And it was all chewed up.**

'I found it in the swamp.'

Until that moment, I'd never believed that anything bad could have happened to Dad. Not Dad. But when I looked at that hat, my insides went cold and I felt sick.

Piper gulped. 'I'm sorry, Ollie,' she said. 'I really am.' Grandma snatched the hat. She examined it closely. 'You're jumping to conclusions,' she said. 'Yes, it is a tiny bit nibbled – but that doesn't mean a croc was responsible. It may have been a koala.'

'A koala?' Mum said.

'Definitely,' said Grandma. 'They're very greedy creatures. They'll eat anything.'

'Really?' I said. I looked at Grandma. Was she serious, or just trying to make us feel better?

'Yes, and anyway, this is a woolly hat. He wouldn't have been wearing it in this heat. It must have fallen out of the plane when he crashed.'

My heart did a little bounce. **SHE WAS RIGHT.**

Dad didn't like hats anyway. Especially the ones Mum knitted. He said they were itchy.

Mum shook her head. 'Where is he then?' she said. 'Why can't we find him?'

Grandma shrugged. 'Maybe he bumped his head and lost his sense of direction.' She turned to me. 'Did he sound dizzy when he phoned?'

I thought back to the call. 'Not particularly,' I said.

'Well, there must be **some** explanation.' Grandma stood up. 'Your father's an **outstanding** explorer. It wouldn't be like him to get lost.'

'Exactly,' howled Mum. 'He's been eaten, and it's all my fault.'

'How exactly is it your fault?' Piper asked.

'I should never have let him go. I should have put my foot down. I knew it would be dangerous.'

Piper raised her eyebrows. 'To be fair, Ollie's mum, you think walking to the shop is dangerous. Ollie's been at least twice since you've been away and look, he's fine.'

'To the shop? By himself?' Mum looked horrified. 'He's only eleven.'

Grandma elbowed Piper in the ribs. 'Ha – she's having you on,' she said. 'Believe me, Sukey, I stuck to your list like glue. I made completely sure that Ollie never went anywhere without an adult, he's eaten nothing but high-fibre, unprocessed foods, revision every night, there have been no animals sleeping in your bed—'

'I don't remember that being on my list,' Mum said.

'Wasn't it?' Grandma said. 'That's good.'

I stood up and reached for Rose. 'Can we go?' I said. 'It's getting dark.'

Mum scrambled to her feet. 'Do you really think he's still alive?' she asked.

'I've never been surer of anything,' Grandma said. 'Seriously.'

Mum grabbed her rucksack. 'Which way, then, Florence?'

'Back to the hotel.' Grandma picked up her bag.

'Come on. No time to lose.'

Mum looked doubtful. 'Really?' she said. 'Shouldn't we just carry on looking?'

'Not in the dark,' Grandma said. 'It'd be a total disaster.'

Mum nodded. 'You're right. Of course you are.'

'Anyway.' Grandma marched ahead. 'Bruce is cooking me supper. I'm looking forward to it.'

32

Bruce looked surprised to see Mum with us. 'You found her so quickly!' he said. 'That's ... um ... fantastic. Yes. FANTASTIC.'

He ran around the hotel hammering on doors.

'They're back. They're back,' he shouted. 'They've found the mother! And a hat! **Sensational!'**

A few reporters came out and mooched about, but they didn't seem that interested. One or two took pictures of Mum, but then she went to bed.

'All that fuss, I thought they'd found at least a limb,' I heard one mutter. 'A chewed bobble hat will only sell so many papers. I'm off home in the morning.'

'That won't please Bruce,' Piper said, when I told her. 'He's counting on the reporters to keep the hotel going.'

'We'll be here till we find Dad.' I hoped Grandma

hadn't given all our money away. We'd need some to pay the bill. I peered into the crowded dining room. Bruce was in there talking to a news crew. 'I expect this is the busiest the hotel has ever been.'

'Is that Bert and Ed?' Piper grabbed my arm. 'It is. Look. There, at the bar. I thought they were going straight to the airfield?'

'They've seen us,' I said. **'They're coming over.'**

'Evening, Ollie.' Bert clapped me hard on the back. Ow. 'How's your furry mouse thing?'

I felt inside my pocket. Myrtle was still there, curled up, asleep. 'She's fine,' I said. 'Thanks for rescuing her.'

'Our flight's not till nine thirty,' Ed said. 'We thought we'd pop in. Say hello. Have a bit of a clean-up.'

'Couldn't you find the bathroom?' Piper asked.

Bert ignored her, and looked around, casually. 'Where's your gran, Ollie? It'd be nice to say goodbye to her and the little doggy before we leave.'

'I think she went to check on Mum,' I said.

'Would that be down this corridor?' Bert craned his neck. A bit of dried mud flaked off it. 'If we miss her, pass on our best, won't you?'

'OK,' I said. I watched as they walked away. I still wasn't convinced they were Scout leaders. I hoped they weren't up to anything.

'Bruce is waving,' Piper said. 'I think he wants you.'

I looked over. What was he wearing? He looked like he was going to a wedding in his cream suit and cravat. He must be ever so hot. His moustache was drooping and he kept dabbing the shine off his forehead with large powder puff.

'Ollie?' he called. 'Ollie? I need a word and you're on in five.' He held up his hand with his fingers spread.

What did he mean? On in five? On what in five? I walked across to see what he was talking about.

'On live TV, Ollie! In five minutes.' Bruce clapped his hands together. 'This is SO exciting! Did I hear your mum went to bed?' He tutted. 'Almost a shame she turned up. The press were much more interested with them both missing. Go and get her, Ollie, this is important.' He gave a little hop. 'The cameras are all set up. Darwin TV are about to broadcast live to the nation.'

'Broadcast what?'

'Three generations united in grief. You and your mum and your gran.' Bruce was quivering with excitement. **'I can't believe my humble hotel is going to be on national news.'**

I stared at Bruce in disbelief. 'Dad's not dead,' I said. 'He's missing. We don't know that anything bad has happened to him.'

'It probably has. All you found was a piece of his hat.'

'Grandma said—'

'Never mind what your gran said. Your dad's put this place on the map.' He looked around to see if anyone was listening, and lowered his voice. 'I mean, call me callous, but one has to seize an opportunity when one can.'

'What are you talking about?' I said.

Bruce reached out and held me by the shoulders. 'Ollie. In five minutes you're going to be on live TV, talking to the **world**. All you have to do is say what a great man your dad was and how much you miss him.'

'Eh?'

'You can show them the hat – let them get a good close-up – **and then you need to tell them about the diamond.'**

'What diamond?'

'The one your dad was carrying in his plane. The **enormous** one, worth a king's ransom.'

Eh? A diamond? What was Bruce talking about? I shook my head. 'He didn't have a diamond,' I said.

Bruce took me by the shoulders. 'Well, I know that and YOU know that – but nobody else does, see?'

I didn't see at all. I stared at him. Bruce was completely loopy.

'Why do you want me to pretend he was carrying a diamond?'

'There's something in it for both of us, Ollie.' He leant closer and lowered his voice. 'The press are losing interest in your dad. It's yesterday's news. If you tell them about the diamond—'

'There is no diamond,' I said.

'Whatever, Ollie, whatever. Anyway. As I was saying, if you tell them about the diamond, we'll be inundated with treasure hunters from across the globe! They'll all be looking for the swamp where your dad's plane went down! Do you see?'

'But what's the point?'

'What's the point? They'll need somewhere to stay, and where better than here?' He gesticulated wildly. 'I'll be able to expand. Maybe get a hot tub? An outside seating area? The possibilities are endless.'

'You want me to lie so you can get a hot tub?'

'It's only a teeny lie, Ollie.' He clasped his hands. 'Everyone lies sometimes.'

I know that. Of course everyone lies sometimes. I lied about eating the grub, and Mum lied about Great Aunt Lucy – and Grandma lied because she didn't want to share her biscuits. But this didn't seem the same. It didn't seem the same at all.

'I'm sorry.' I shook my head. 'I can't make something up so you can rent out a few more rooms.'

'But people will come to search. One of them is bound to find your dad, dead or alive. Do it for him, if not for me? Think about it, at least?'

I didn't need to think about it. 'No,' I said. 'I won't. **You're crazy.** And we don't need your help any more. I'll find Dad myself.'

I turned and walked away. Bruce could do his press conference and make up whatever stories he liked. I didn't want anything to do with it. He wasn't bothered about Dad at all! He only cared about his stupid hotel, and being on the telly, and getting a hot tub!!!!

I stomped out into the back yard and found a step to sit on. Even though it was dark, it was still boiling. I swatted at a fly and pulled my top away from my skin. **I HATED THE HEAT.** I definitely didn't have explorer genes. I decided to work extra hard at maths when I got back to school. **I might even put my name down for work experience at the bank.**

Bruce's voice started to bellow out from inside. I wondered what rubbish he was spouting for the cameras.

Poor Dad. Where was he? Maybe he'd rescued himself? Perhaps, as we'd been heading to Australia in the balloon, he'd been heading for home? He'd get back and wonder where we all were. He'd find the house in a bit of a mess. I should have left a note.

Dear Dad,

We have gone to look for you. If you are back before us, could you clear up a bit, as Mum will go crazy.

Look forward to seeing you.

Lots of love,

Ollie xx

I sighed. If he'd flown home, he'd have been in touch by now, to let us know he was safe. He'd have called, or emailed, or something. Bruce was right. Something bad had happened. A tear trickled down my cheek. I tried to think about the good things. At least we'd found Mum. And I'd got lovely Myrtle back. I reached into my pocket and pulled her out. She was so cute and fluffy – I couldn't imagine being without her. Poor thing, she'd been cooped up all day. I bet she was missing her wheel.

I was just sitting there watching her scamper around my lap, when Rose sauntered out the back door. That wasn't good. Myrtle didn't like Rose, for obvious reasons. I tried to shove her back into my pocket, but it was too late. They'd seen each other.

'Myrtle! No!' I tried to grab her as she made a leap for it, but she was too quick. Rose was pretty fast too. He shot after her, yapping furiously.

I sprang to my feet. I had to catch them. Cats might have nine lives but I was pretty sure hamsters didn't. If Rose ate Myrtle I wouldn't be able to bear it. Where were they? There! I could just see them through the gloom, zigzagging through the grass. Rose was snapping ferociously and Myrtle was a whisker ahead.

'ROSE!' I yelled. **'STOP!'** I pulled my torch from

my pocket and flicked it on. It wasn't very bright. I should have changed the batteries. Was that them? Yes! Over by the outbuilding – the one Piper thought the pool might be in.

By the time I got there, Rose was scratching frantically at the door. Myrtle must have run underneath. Thank goodness! She was safe.

I ran up and glared at Rose. He might have found Mum, but chasing Myrtle like that was no way to behave. 'You're disgraceful,' I said. 'You'd better go back to the hotel.'

Rose hung his head in shame.

'Go on,' I pointed. 'Go and find Grandma.'

He slunk off the veranda and up the path. I watched till he'd gone inside. I wasn't going to risk him racing back the minute Myrtle stuck her nose out.

I tried the door, but it was locked. I knelt down to peer underneath but I couldn't see a thing. 'Myrtle?' I hissed. 'Myrtle?'

I listened. Nothing.

I felt above the doorframe to see if there was a key, and looked under a broken flowerpot, but there wasn't one. I stepped back and shone my torch down the side of the building. There was a load of junk piled down there – and hey! **The outbuilding had a window!** It was only a small one, and quite high up, but if I stood on that pile of paving slabs, I'd be able to see in.

I glanced back towards the hotel. It had gone quiet. The press conference must have finished. I didn't want Bruce to catch me snooping. I was probably OK, though. Grandma had said he was cooking her supper. He was probably flambéing something. I shuddered. What did she see in him? He was awful.

I climbed on to the slabs and shone my torch through the dusty glass. It wasn't a pool house. Definitely not. It was where Bruce stored all his old junk. There was loads of it. I could make out fence posts, a bedstead, a cupboard and – yay! MYRTLE! There she was! Scuttling chubbily across the floor. What was that she'd just run underneath? Something huge, covered in tarpaulin. What was it? An old truck?

I pointed my torch directly at it.

Eh? The shape seemed familiar – really familiar. I blinked. That couldn't be right. I must be imagining things. I'd be able to see better if the glass wasn't so grimy. I rubbed at the pane, and tried tugging at the window, but it didn't budge. Then, just to make things even trickier, my torch flickered and went out.

I climbed down from the paving slabs and sat on them in the dark. It couldn't be what I thought it was. It just couldn't. It didn't make sense.

I'd need to get inside to check. I looked back up at the window. Maybe I could lever it open? I might be able to fit through it.

'Ollie?'

I almost jumped out of my skin!

It was Piper. 'Don't sneak up,' I said. 'You scared the life out of me.'

She switched on her torch and shone it in my face. 'Rose came in without you. I was worried.'

'I'm fine,' I said. I pushed the torch away.

'Were you looking for the swimming pool? I thought you said there wasn't one?'

I shook my head. 'It's Myrtle. Rose chased her in.'

'Is she OK?' Piper asked.

'She's fine.'

Piper flicked her torch back at me. 'So if she's all right, why are you looking so weird?'

I pointed up at the window. 'There's something in there.'

Piper giggled. 'What?' she said. 'A ghost?'

I took a deep breath.

'A plane.'

34

Piper looked at me like I was mad. 'A plane?' she said. 'In there?'

'Yes.'

'OMG,' Piper said. 'Your dad's plane?'

'I don't know,' I said. 'It's covered up.'

'It can't be your dad's plane.' She sounded incredulous. **'Why would it be in Bruce's shed?'**

I shrugged. 'He might have found it.'

Piper shook her head. 'No,' she said. 'He would have told us. Why would he not tell us?'

We looked at each other. I gulped. What was Bruce up to? 'Where is he now?' I asked. We both turned and looked towards the hotel.

'Ollie.' Piper grabbed my arm. 'I think someone's coming out.'

'Turn your torch off,' I hissed. 'Quick.'

We stood in the dark. We didn't move. The door to the hotel creaked, and then swung open.

It was Bruce.

He stood there, silhouetted in the doorway. 'Ollie?' he called. 'And ... um ... the other one? You're not out here, are you? Remember the snakes?'

He stared out across the yard. I felt a bit sick. If that was Dad's plane in there, Bruce had hidden it for a reason.

He stepped out into the yard and softly closed the door behind him.

'What's he carrying?' Piper whispered. 'It looks like a basket. Maybe he's planning a picnic for your gran.'

'Shhhh.' I elbowed her. He was heading straight for us! I took a step backwards. 'Get down,' I whispered. 'Behind the paving slabs.'

We crouched there as his footsteps got closer, crunching across the yard and rustling through the grass. Why was he here?

I heard a rattle and a click. Bruce must be opening the outbuilding. Was he looking for us? I didn't move. I couldn't breathe. I felt Piper stiffen next to me.

'He's gone inside,' she whispered. 'I hope he doesn't step on Myrtle.'

So did I. What was he doing? I could hear him moving about, but then there was silence.

Not for long.

Bang. The back door to the hotel flew open.

'BRUCE? BRUCE?'

It was Grandma!

'Bruce?' she shouted. 'Are you out there? Bruce?'

There was some thudding and Bruce reappeared,

muttering. I made out a couple of words. They weren't very polite. 'On my way, Florence,' he called. 'Just dealing with some rattlers.'

'I need to borrow your truck,' Grandma bellowed. 'It's Rose! **He's been stolen!**'

'Your darling little pup?' Bruce started running towards the hotel. 'Who would do such a terrible thing?'

'Bert and Ed. That's who.' Grandma was furious. 'They came to say goodbye, and I haven't seen Rose since. The cheek of it. I gave them plenty of money for their roof, the double-crossing scoundrels. I'll be reporting them to the Chief Scout. Come on. We'll catch them at the airfield.'

'I'm right behind you, Florence,' Bruce said. He ran in through the door and slammed it shut. A few seconds later his truck roared into life and sped away.

Piper turned her torch back on. 'I wonder if it counts as stealing, if you're stealing something back?'

'Whose side are you on?' I asked. 'Grandma gave

them all that money so she could keep Rose.'

'I told her not to.' Piper waved her torch. 'Come on. Bruce is out of the way. We need to get into this building.'

I looked back up at the window. 'You're smaller than me,' I said. 'You could get through there, couldn't you?'

'I'm not squeezing through that. I might get stuck,' Piper said. She walked around to the front of the outbuilding, and I followed her. 'I'll see if I can pick the lock,' she said. 'Have you got a hairgrip?'

I looked at her. Was she kidding? **'Of course I haven't,'** I said.

'You might have done. You're a Scout, aren't you? Aren't you supposed to "be prepared"?'

'Not for burglary,' I said. 'They don't encourage that.'

'Well, there's only one way in then,' Piper said. 'We'll have to break it down. Hold this, will you?' She handed me the torch and took a step back.

'Wait.'

'Ollie, we need to get in. It doesn't matter if it's a little bit against the law.'

'It's not that,' I said. 'Look.' I gave the door a push. It swung open.

'OMG! Ollie!' Piper clapped her hands. 'He left it unlocked! How **lucky** is that?'

'We'd better hurry.' I said. 'It's not far to the airfield. They could be back soon.'

I shone the torch in first. It didn't look very inviting. I'd never seen so much junk. And it smelt of damp, and oil, and mice. And there were so many cobwebs. I shuddered and tried not to think about spiders. Piper gave me a shove.

'I thought you said to hurry,' she said.

I stepped inside. 'Keep an eye out for Myrtle,' I said. **'Don't tread on her.'**

Piper followed me. 'I'll close the door,' she said. 'In case Bruce comes back.'

'Good idea.' I didn't want to think what he'd do if he found us.

'So.' Piper stepped over some old boxes and squeezed past a cupboard. She looked around. 'Where's the plane?'

'Over there.' I pointed the torch. 'See.'

Piper walked towards it. 'It's definitely big enough.' She stood and looked up at it. Then she looked at me. 'Go on, then. Pull the cover off.'

I stepped forward, but then I hesitated. If it was Dad's plane, **what would that mean?**

'Oh, for goodness sake.' Piper shoved me out of the way and gave the tarpaulin a mighty tug. It slid to the floor.

WOW. There it stood, gleaming in the torchlight.

'It's definitely a plane,' Piper said. 'Is it his?'

'Yes,' I said. 'It is.'

I swallowed hard. The last time I'd seen it, Dad had been sitting in it, waving at me.

Piper walked around and inspected it. 'There's hardly a scratch on it,' she said. 'The landing gear's a bit buckled, but that's all.'

'But how did it get here?' I said. 'Why didn't Bruce say?' Piper reached up and spun the propeller. 'He needs money. Perhaps he thought that when the fuss died down, he'd be able to sell it?'

'But **he** was the one making the fuss,' I said. 'Inviting the press and everything.'

'He must have felt bad your dad was still out there.'

'I'm not sure Bruce is the sort of person who'd feel bad about anything,' I said.

Piper held out her hand for the torch. She climbed up and peered into the cockpit. 'It all seems odd. Fair enough, your dad crashed – but then he got lost. From what you've said, it doesn't seem like him.' She leant into the plane. 'Hey! Look.' She held something up. **'Is this his phone?'**

She handed it down. I stared at it. It **W𝖆S** Dad's phone. I didn't understand. 'He called us from this after the crash,' I said. 'From a tree. He didn't leave it in the plane.'

'Maybe he dropped it? Bruce might have picked it up?'

'Maybe.' I had a go at switching it on, but it was dead. I passed it back. 'Let's charge it. At least we'll be able to see when he used it last.'

Piper looked at me. 'Is there a charger at the hotel?'

'There's one built into the dashboard. There.' I pointed. 'Next to the joystick.'

'Oh, right.' She plugged it in and I heard a soft **ping**. 'OK,' she said. 'What shall we do while we're waiting?'

'We should get out of here, for a start,' I said. 'And as soon as Grandma gets back, we'll tell her about the plane.'

'What about Myrtle?' Piper jumped down.

'Should we look for her?'

'She'll be all right,' I said. 'She'll have made a nest somewhere. I'll find her later.'

'If you're sure.' Piper walked to the door and pulled at the handle. Then she pulled harder.

She turned to look at me. There was panic on her face.

'Ollie, it won't open.'

35

I **tried the** door again, just in case she hadn't pulled hard enough, but it wouldn't budge. 'It must be one of those self-locking doors,' I said. 'We shouldn't have shut it.'

'It wouldn't be good if Bruce found us in here,' Piper said. 'He'd have to silence us. Feed us to **wombats** or something.'

'Thanks, Piper,' I said. 'That's a nice thought.'

'Tell you what. We'll lie in wait.' She pointed her torch at a pile of posts in the corner. 'Grab one of those. When he comes in, you can **wallop** him.'

I wasn't convinced. Bruce was a lot bigger than me. I looked up at the window. 'Come on, Piper. It unlocks from this side. You'd definitely fit.'

She wasn't keen. It took me ages to persuade her, and to be honest, it was a bit of a squeeze. Thinking about it, **she probably shouldn't have gone headfirst**, but it wasn't that far to the ground, and she didn't knock herself out or anything.

She scrambled to her feet. 'The truck's not back,' she said. 'I'll go and see if I can find a spare key. Shall I leave you the torch? I know you don't like the dark.'

'Ha ha,' I said. 'Funny.'

'OK,' Piper said. 'I'll see you in a bit.'

I am **not** afraid of the dark, **definitely** not, but even so, once Piper had gone, I did feel a bit uneasy, what with all the shadows and rustling of spiders. Perhaps I should arm myself with a bit of fence? I tried to remember where it was. Somewhere near the door? I kept tripping over things. Then I stubbed my toe on the corner of the old cupboard. OW. Maybe I should go and sit in the plane? At least it was comfy.

I felt my way across and climbed up into the cockpit. Dad's phone was lying on the instrument panel where Piper had left it. I picked it up and switched it on. **Yay** – it was already half charged! I checked for a signal, but there wasn't one, so I couldn't call Grandma – but I could at least search for clues. I mean, if he'd taken pictures of the crash site, we could try and work out where it was.

I started to look through his photos. **Ha ha** – there was a great selfie of him and me that we took just before he left – and one of him and Mum that I'd taken, and – *oh* – I must have taken the next three by accident, because they were of my feet.

The next **two hundred million** pictures were ones that Dad had taken from the plane and were **really** boring.

I kept flicking through until I got to the very last shot.

Eh?

I peered closely at the screen.

What?

It was a picture of Dad. **With Bruce.**

36

Bruce had his arm around Dad's shoulders, and they were both grinning into the lens. The plane was gleaming in the background –

and behind the plane was Humpty Doo Towers. **Dad had been here! He'd been here with Bruce!** I looked at the date. The day of the crash! Dad hadn't been eaten by crocs at all! He'd been here long enough to get to know Bruce and take a photo.

I didn't understand. **Why hadn't he called to tell us he was safe?** There was a landline at the hotel.

Why hadn't Bruce told anyone?

Where was Dad? What had Bruce done with him?

I started to tremble. I needed to get out of here. I'd take a fence post and **smash** my way out if I had to. I went to put the phone down, and as I did, I noticed something. Something on the screen. Next to the messaging app.

A tiny exclamation mark.

Oh my.

I knew what it meant. It meant that Dad had written a text, and it hadn't sent.

I took a deep breath and tapped the screen.

There were three. Three messages. All to Mum.

Hi, Sukey!

Hope you get this. Just to let you know I'm fine. Met a local who helped me get my plane out of the swamp. Owns a hotel. I'll stay for a couple of days until the engine's fixed.

Love to Ollie.

Henry xx

The next was pretty short.

Change of plan. This guy is crazy. Leaving as soon as I can.

The third was just one word.

Help!!!!

I sat there and stared at the screen. **Bruce really was a bad guy.** I leant my head back against the seat. What had he done? More importantly, **what had he done to *Dad*?**

Then I heard something.

I sat bolt upright.

Footsteps?

Were those footsteps?

I held my breath and listened. Yes. They were. Walking round outside. What should I do? I couldn't hide in the cockpit – it was too small. Where, then? That cupboard? Was it big enough? Probably. I started to climb down from the plane. Very, very quietly.

Then I stopped. What was I thinking? **I wasn't going to hide.**

I tiptoed my way to the pile of fence posts, and then I grabbed one and crept over to the door. I was going to get Bruce. **I was going to make him tell me everything he knew.**

'Hello!' Piper stuck her head in through the window. 'I couldn't find a key.'

I almost had a heart attack! **'Don't DO that,'** I said crossly.

'Sorry. You'll never guess, Ollie.'

I put the fence post down. 'What?'

'I've got Rose.' She held him up. 'He was asleep on the bed.' She giggled. 'He must have escaped from Bert and Ed all by himself.'

'Can you come back in?' I said. 'I need to show you something.'

'Are you all right?' Piper said.

'Not really,' I said.

She shone her torch at me. 'Blimey, Ollie. You look **dreadful**. Here. Take Rose.' she passed him through. 'I'll come in backwards. Head-first wasn't dignified.'

Backwards wasn't very dignified either. Normally, I would have mentioned it, but I wasn't in the mood. She dropped down on to the floor next to me. 'Go on then, what is it?'

I gave her the phone. 'Read those,' I said.

'Oh right. OK.'

For a moment, she didn't say anything at all. She sort of blinked a bit and then she shook her head.

'**Wow,**' she said. 'Bruce, eh?' Then she paused. 'Oh well,' she said. 'At least we know your dad made it out of the bush. He's here somewhere, dead or alive.'

'That's good to know,' I said. 'Thanks. Any bright ideas as to where he might be?'

Piper shrugged. 'I guess we'll have to ask Bruce,' she said.

Rose had started to scrabble. He wanted to get down. I hung on to him. Was it Bruce this time? I glanced towards the door.

'It's Myrtle!' Piper pointed. 'He's seen Myrtle! Look, there she goes!'

Yay! Myrtle!

She scurried across the floor and vanished under the cupboard. Rose struggled frantically. He couldn't help himself. He was desperate to eat her. In the end, we had to strap him into the plane. He sat there on Dad's seat and glowered at us.

'Leave him,' I said. 'Let's rescue Myrtle.'

The cupboard was heavier than it looked. We

couldn't move it at all. Piper got on her hands and knees and peered underneath. 'It's bolted to the floor,' she said. 'Why would it be bolted to the floor?'

I shrugged. Who knew. Bruce was nuts. I pulled the cupboard door open. 'I'll see if I can lift out a plank and get to Myrtle that way,' I said.

Eh? That was weird. There wasn't a bottom to the cupboard.

No bottom.

No bottom at all.

There was a hole. And steps. Stone steps. **Going down.**

37

Piper blinked. **'Well,'** she said. 'They'll lead somewhere, won't they?

'Yep,' I said.

'Who's going first?' she said.

'I will,' I said. 'Give me your torch.'

It turned out I didn't need the torch. There was a click, and the overhead lights came on.

'Piper!' I hissed. **'Turn them off!'**

'It wasn't me,' Piper said. 'I didn't touch anything.'

Oh.

We looked at each other, and then we turned around.

It was Bruce. Of *course* it was.

He was just standing there, in his grubby cream suit, watching us. Rose was tucked under his arm. He must have crept over and unstrapped him.

'Carry on,' Bruce said. He gave a high-pitched giggle. 'Don't let me stop you.'

'Rose could have warned us,' Piper muttered. 'So much for being a teller of fortune.' I looked around for the fence post, but I'd left it by the door. I glared at Bruce. 'Is my dad down there?' I pointed down the steps.

Bruce took a step closer. A tiny bead of sweat dripped from his nose, and landed on Rose.

'You're just like him, Ollie.' He shook his head mournfully. 'He wouldn't go along with my plan either.'

'What plan?' I said. 'He's all right, isn't he?'

Bruce sighed. 'He only had to stay hidden for a **few** weeks, to get people worried. Then I was going to rescue him. Can you imagine the publicity? He wouldn't even consider it.'

I gazed at him in bewilderment. 'But why?' I said. **'What was the point?'**

'My time on *Bush Oyster Buffet* was the best of my life, Ollie. I was famous – recognised on the street, asked for autographs.' Bruce wiped away a tear. 'The fame didn't last – but I bought this place and I had a vision for it. Champagne and cocktails and celebrities in hot tubs.' He gestured wildly.

'It's not really the sort of place celebrities would come to,' Piper said. 'It's not very classy.'

'It could have been, but I ran out of money. I needed more. No one was coming to stay. I'd been forgotten. I haven't been on daytime TV in years. I had to raise my profile, get my face on the front of a few papers. And when your dad walked out of the trees – it seemed like the ideal opportunity.'

'But he said no,' I said.

'He laughed at me. He said I was nuts, Ollie. **NUTS**.'

Piper took a step forward. 'You're not nuts, Bruce.

Of course you're not.'

Eh? What was she on about? Bruce was clearly quite ma—

Piper elbowed me. 'Ollie. Bruce isn't nuts, is he?'

'Um, actually, I'd say he—'

Bruce's eyes started to narrow. Piper elbowed me harder.

Oh. Right. I got it. 'Of course you're not nuts, Bruce,' I said. **'Not at all.'**

Bruce's moustache drooped down at the corners. 'It's very hurtful,' he said, 'when people **laugh** at you.'

'I can imagine, Bruce.' Piper reached out and patted his arm. 'Do you want to tell us about it?'

Bruce hung his head. 'I was so cross.'

Piper raised her eyebrows. 'What did you do, Bruce?'

'Well,' Bruce muttered. 'He said he wanted to leave, but he'd run out of peanut oil. I told him there was some in the cellar. Down he went, and I shut him in. Simple.'

'Then what?' I said.

'Well, I waited for him to be reported missing, and then I emailed your mum, Ollie. Her name was in the papers. I got her address from the council website.' He looked smug. 'Clever, eh?'

'Genius,' Piper said. 'I wouldn't have thought of that.'

'Anyway.' Bruce scowled. 'By the time she got out here, the press were losing interest in your dad. Explorers go missing round here all the time.'

'Really?' I said.

'They usually turn up. **Sometimes in bits**, sometimes not. So I decided it would be good if your mum went missing too. I told her to follow the path which led to my crocodile traps. **Bingo!**' Bruce preened. 'The press descended again. **It was wonderful.**'

'Wow,' said Piper admiringly. 'What a plan!'

'Yes, until you lot found her. That was annoying, I must say.'

'Is Dad all right?' I asked. 'Not hurt, or anything?'

Bruce shrugged. 'He's fine. It's a nice cellar. There's a skylight and a sofa. He's got **loads** of sandwiches and a copy of *Hello*. He's a good bloke, actually. Said he'd design me a possum trap. I've been taking him materials.'

I closed my eyes in relief. Thank goodness. **Dad was OK.**

'What were you planning on doing with him?' Piper said. 'Did you think he'd change his mind?'

Bruce looked sulky. 'I hadn't really thought it through,' he said. 'And now you two have to go down there with him. Honestly. You're so inconvenient.'

'How about you just let us all go home?' said Piper. 'We won't tell anyone.'

Bruce's eyebrows shot up. 'Of course you will,' he said. 'I'm not an **idiot**. You'll sell your story for thousands!'

'No, we wouldn't,' I said. **'Not everyone wants to be famous.'**

Bruce gave a little giggle. 'Don't be ridiculous,' he said. 'Of course they do. Now hurry up – I've got to go and announce you're missing. Down you go. Here. Take Fido with you.' He shoved Rose into my arms. 'Look at him. What a mutt. What on earth did you bring him along fo—' He suddenly stopped and looked thoughtful. 'What was that you said earlier?' he said.

'When?'

'This morning. At the press conference? About him being magic, or something? What was it you called him?' He paused. 'Ah! That was it. *A Dog of Destiny*.'

'It's just a rumour,' I said. 'I'm pretty sure he's not.'

Bruce gave a little hop. 'I bet he is! Your gran was **furious** when those Scout chaps took him.' He tittered. 'Luckily for them, they were just taking off when your gran turned up, or I don't know what would have happened. They shouted out something about the dog having run away. Your gran wasn't happy, I can tell you. Thought I'd never hear the end of it. And look! After all that, here he is.'

'Where's Grandma now?' I asked.

'Eating her supper. I'm an excellent cook. Good healthy food. I was a bit worried about where you two had got to, so I told her I was going to the loo. Now. Come on, **hand over the pooch.**'

'No,' I said.

'Come on. Think of the possibilities! I'll get my own show!' He clapped like an excited seal. 'I can see it now! Up in lights! **Brilliant Bruce and his Wonderful Woofer. I'll be a STAR** again.' He stood there, moustache quivering, gazing into the distance.

Piper and I looked at each other and then at the door. Could we make a run for it? Should we? Was it too risky? **And what about Dad?** He was still down in the cellar. We couldn't leave him.

'I'll run,' Piper whispered. 'I'll take Rose. He'll try to stop me. You let your dad out.'

I nodded.

'Go!' Piper snatched Rose and sprinted for the

door. Bruce started from his daydream and tore after her. This was my chance!

I turned and threw myself into the cupboard, slamming the door shut behind me. I probably shouldn't have done that. I could hardly see a thing and the steps were ever so steep. I felt for the first one, and then the second. There weren't many – a dozen or so – and then they levelled out and stopped at a door.

Oh my. I couldn't believe it. It didn't have a proper lock! There was just a bolt.

I slid it back and pushed. It was **eerily** quiet. I could hear my breath. It was so dark. Dark and silent. 'Dad?' I whispered. 'Dad?'

Nothing.

I stepped inside.

Something grabbed me by the leg! I had no time to react. None at all. Whatever it was jerked me upwards! Eh? I was hanging upside down! How on earth did that happen? And what was this net?

'Hey,' I yelled. 'Hey!'
Suddenly the lights came
on. Ow, that was bright!
I squinted.
'OLLIE?'
I might have known.
'DAD!' I said.
Dad untangled me
from his possum trap
and it was really great to
see him. Like, **really**
really great. I think Dad was pleased to see me as
well, but mainly he just looked amazed.

'Does Mum know you're here?' he asked. 'I can't
believe she let you come.'

'I'll explain later,' I said. 'Come on. We have to
rescue Piper.'

'Who?' Dad said.

'You know. Piper from school. She came to help.
Bruce probably caught her.'

'He certainly did.' Bruce bustled triumphantly through the doorway. He had Rose draped over his shoulder and was shoving Piper in front of him. 'She's not very nice,' he said. 'She kicked me.'

'I don't blame her,' I said. **'You're bonkers.'**

'No need to be rude,' Bruce said. 'Anyway. I'm going to lock you all in here while I finalise my new plan.'

'You can't leave us for too long,' Piper said. 'It's hot. Ollie will drive me mad with all his complaining.'

'Well, you've only got yourself to blame,' Bruce said. 'Nosing around. I **told** you not to pry.' He gave Piper a little push and she stumbled over to join us. 'Right.' Bruce started to head out the door. 'We're off. By the time I let you out, Rose and I will be superstars. No one will believe a word you say.'

I looked up at Dad. There were three of us. I mean, Bruce was pretty big, but surely we could take him down. 'Piper?' I hissed. 'Come on.'

Dad grabbed my shoulder. 'Ollie,' he said. 'Don't. You might get hurt.'

253

Blimey. He was as bad as Mum! Didn't he want to get out of here?

Piper bent down and picked up a piece of wood that had been part of the possum trap. 'Come on, Ollie,' she said. 'Let's get him.'

I wriggled out of Dad's grip and reached for another plank.

Eh? What was Bruce doing?

He'd stopped in the doorway and seemed to be doing a little dance. Then he gave a loud squawk and started to smack his leg.

'It's a rat!' Bruce slapped wildly. 'A rat ran up my trousers! I saw it! **Help! HELP! I hate rats!'**

Rose's ears pricked up. He started scrabbling. Bruce tried to hang on to him with one arm but it was no good. Rose was going CRAZY! He sprang from Bruce's grip and landed at his feet. Oh my! I'd never seen a dog so small quite so savage. He jumped and he snarled and he nipped and nipped at the material of Bruce's suit.

'Good for you, Rose,' I shouted. **'Go for it.'**

'Get him off me!' Bruce had gone quite purple. He shook his leg in the air. Rose hung on grimly. **'Get him OFF!'**

'Oh, for goodness sake,' Piper said. She lifted her plank and whacked Bruce on the knee. I think she was hoping to knock him off balance, but he was so busy wrestling with Rose, he barely noticed. She raised the plank again.

'Careful, Piper,' Dad said anxiously. 'He might be litigious.'

This time Bruce saw her coming. He grabbed the plank and tried to wrench it away from her. Oh no! She was being swung all over the place!

'Let go,' I shouted.

She did. **Ow.**

'Soz,' Piper said, sitting up. 'He was stronger than I thought.'

Bruce was slapping again. 'It's still up my trousers,' he shrieked. 'It's scampering about! It's in my pants!

Someone get it out!'

Rose snarled and savaged Bruce's leg again.

'Ollie! Quick!' Dad held up the netting from the possum trap. 'This should do it. Take the other end.'

'Got it.'

Piper saw what we were going to do. She grabbed Rose and whisked him out of the way. *'Now,'* she shouted.

Dad and I stretched the net tight and ran full pelt at Bruce.

To be honest, he was in such a frenzy it wasn't hard to wrap him up. Once he realised what we were doing he did struggle a bit but it was no good. By then his arms were pinned against his sides and he couldn't move his legs.

'You won't get away with this,' he screeched.

'I think we might, actually,' said Piper. She gave him a little push, and he overbalanced on to the floor with a satisfying thud.

Then we sat on him.

'There you are!' Grandma appeared in the doorway. 'What on earth are you doing to Bruce? Are you having a bundle? Can anyone play?'

Then she noticed Dad. And Rose. I'm not sure who she was more pleased to see, to be honest.

It took a while for me to explain the full story, especially with Bruce interrupting non-stop.

'Get the rat,' he kept bellowing. **'It's tickling.'**

Grandma was not impressed once she'd heard what had happened. Not at all.

'I'm **very disappointed** in you, Bruce,' she said. **'Very.'** Then she trod on his hand. She said it was an accident, but it probably wasn't.

'What shall we do about the rat?' I asked.

'Leave it where it is,' said Grandma.

'Noooo,' roared Bruce.

'We can't. That would be cruel,' Piper said. 'It must be hideous up there. Look. I've found a bit of sandwich. It's cheese. Rats like cheese. I'll coax him out.' She knelt down and waved it around Bruce's ankles.

His turn-ups twitched. A nose appeared, followed by some furry cheeks.

'That's not a rat!' I shouted.

'Isn't it?' Dad said, struggling to hold on to Rose.

'No! It's Myrtle!'

Once Myrtle was safely out, we locked Bruce in the cellar and went back to the hotel. The reporters were beside themselves to see Dad, and when Mum came out of her bedroom to see what was going on, they went completely **barmy**.

Piper giggled. 'There's going to be a picture of your mum **snogging** your dad in all the papers,' she said. 'That'll be embarrassing when you get back to school.'

'Thanks,' I said. 'Weren't you in charge of calling for backup?'

'Oh yes,' Piper said 'Sorry.'

When the police arrived, Grandma led them to the outbuilding. 'I knew he was up to no good,' she said.

'I can always tell a scoundrel, a mile off. What was that? Dinner? Yes, I admit, I did agree to have dinner with him – but needs must. I'd only had a couple of custard creams for lunch. I was starving.'

Bruce really was loopy. He looked totally delighted to see the press pushing and shoving as he was brought out.

'Yoo-hoo,' he called. 'Yes. It's me. Make sure you get my best side, won't you?' He waved wildly as he was stuffed into the back seat of the patrol car.

'Don't miss out,' he shouted out the window. 'Last chance to get your photo. And don't forget. I'll give a full and exclusive interview to the highest bidd—'

He got a bit muffled then, as the policeman wound the window up.

'Look at him,' Grandma

huffed. 'Such a show-off.' She shook her head. 'Shall I tell you what hurt the most, Ollie?' She dabbed her eyes. 'He didn't know me at all.'

'Didn't he?'

'No. You'll never guess what he served up at supper.'

'What?' I said.

She closed her eyes and shuddered. **'Vegetables.'**

38

Piper and I were sitting on the doorstep with our revision books. It was quite warm for the Easter holidays. Mum had already covered us in factor 150, twice.

Piper had been here a lot since we'd got home. I didn't mind. After all, she **had** helped rescue Dad.

She put her maths book down and turned to face me. 'Do you think Rose really is a Dog of Destiny?' she asked. 'Has he got a lucky aura? Or would things have turned out the same, anyway?'

I thought about it. 'I don't know,' I said. 'Winning the money was lucky, I suppose, but he doesn't seem to have done anything **miraculous**. I thought he was supposed to grant people's wishes.'

'Well, perhaps he's not so good at the obvious stuff,' Piper said. 'He might be more subtle than that.

I mean, he sniffed out the balloon in your dad's workshop, didn't he? If he hadn't done that, we might never have got to Australia.'

'I'm not convinced,' I said. 'Sniffing isn't very magical.'

'It's a means to an end.' Piper rummaged in her bag and pulled out a piece of paper. 'He could hardly wave a wand, could he? He wouldn't be able to hold it in his little paws.'

I looked at her. **Was she serious?**

'I'm going to write a list,' she said. 'A list of fantastic things that have happened since Rose turned up,' she went on. 'And then we can decide. Can I borrow your pencil? Thanks.' She started scribbling. 'Right. You found your dad ... and your mum's much less strict now. She sent you out for milk the other day.'

'She did ring the shop to check I'd got there,' I said. 'But it's progress, I suppose.'

'Your gran's **definitely** got her confidence back.'

'I'm not sure she ever really lost that,' I said.

'What else?' Piper chewed the end of my pencil.

'Can you not do that?' I said. 'I don't want your spit on it.'

'Sorry.' She took it out of her mouth.

'Dad sold the design for his engine,' I said. 'He's over the moon. And Bert and Ed got the money for their roof.'

'Ah, yes.' Piper smirked. 'About that. I saw them in the travel agent's yesterday. You know. The one on the high street? They were booking a cruise.'

'A cruise?'

'Yes.' Piper said. 'A luxury one. They paid in cash. So I checked. There is no Scout hut in Little Potton. Bert and Ed aren't Scout leaders. **They're crooks.'**

'I knew it,' I said. 'You'd better not tell Grandma. She'll be really miffed they spent her money on a holiday.'

Piper shrugged. 'She did steal Rose before they'd had a proper go.'

'I suppose,' I said. 'Even so.'

'Bruce got his heart's desire.' Piper wrote his name down. 'He was on the front page of the *Humpty Doo Herald*, for kidnapping your dad. He's famous again.'

'What about you?' I asked.

'I didn't want anything,' she said. She concentrated on her list.

Why had she gone pink? 'There must have been something,' I said.

'OK. I was pleased Mum had missed me.'

'Anything else?'

She went even pinker. 'I'm glad we're friends,' she mumbled.

Eh? Friends? Me and Piper? I supposed we were. I looked at her. She was chewing my pencil again. **Gross**. 'You can keep that,' I said.

'Thanks.'

We sat in silence for a bit.

'I didn't eat that grub,' I said.

'I know.'

I looked at her. 'Do you think I have got any explorer genes?' I asked.

'I expect so,' Piper said, kindly. 'One or two, at least.'

'Maybe I should go on another adventure,' I said. 'Just to see.'

'Maybe.' Piper picked up the list again. 'What about your mum? Anything?'

'I'm back in time to revise for my exams,' I said. 'She's pretty pleased about that. And she's up for **Health and Safety Officer of the Year** again.'

Piper put down my pencil. 'This all has to be more than coincidence, Ollie,' she said. 'I think your gran's right. Rose **is** lucky.'

I didn't reply. I was looking up. Was that ... was that Grandma's balloon?

Woohoo! It was. She was leaning out of the basket and waving at us. Rose was draped over her shoulder, his curls wafting in the breeze.

Yay! I jumped to my feet and waved back. 'Is she **supposed** to be coming down that fast?' Piper asked. 'I'm not sure,' I said. 'But we should probably get out of the way, just in case.'

It was a close one. The basket missed the greenhouse by a whisker and took out the bird table before crashing into Mum's raised beds. Spring onions flew everywhere.

'Hey there, Ollie,' Grandma shouted, as the balloon collapsed around her. She looked around. 'Where's your mother?'

I brushed off some mud. 'We're out of sunblock,' I said. 'She's gone to the shop.'

'Thank goodness for that,' said Grandma. 'What are you up to? I've got an idea.'

'Is it a good one?' I asked.

'Of course it is,' said Grandma. **'Mine always are.'**

THE END

Ollie and Grandma's adventures
continue in the next book,

GRANDMA DANGEROUS
AND THE EGG OF GLORY!

'Sorry?' I said. 'Did I hear that right?'

'I thought you'd be pleased,' Mum said. 'You said you were bored yesterday.' She unfolded the camp bed alongside mine. 'He'll only be here a **week**.'

'But it's Thomas,' I said. '**Thomas.**' I looked at her in horror. 'You know we don't get on.'

'You didn't get along at Christmas.' Mum busied herself with a pillow. 'That was months ago.'

'He'll be just as annoying.' I said. 'Why can't he stay with one of his other cousins?'

Mum looked sheepish. 'They're all busy.'

'I bet they're not.' I said. 'They'll have just said that so they didn't have to listen to him going on and on, ruining their holidays.'

'Don't be mean,' Mum straightened the sheet. 'It must be hard for him. His parents are always away. Boarding school can't be much fun.'

'I don't know about that,' I said. 'Aunt Sarah says it's the best boarding school in the world. Apparently, it's got a one-hundred-metre swimming pool, and Leonardo DiCaprio runs the drama department.'

'She was exaggerating,' Mum said. 'The pool's only fifty metres. I looked on the website.'

Fifty metres is still massive! **My school doesn't even have a paddling pool!** (I suppose there's quite a big tank in the science room, but that has frogspawn in it.)

Mum went on. 'He's doing very well. Sarah says he's top of the class in almost every subject.'

'There's a surprise,' I muttered.

Thomas is the same age as me, but that's the only thing we have in common. **He's ever so annoying.** He spent whole of Christmas putting things on plates and offering them round. If there was a championship in sucking up, he would definitely win it.

Aunt Sarah's always going on about how clever he is. Once, I overheard her say she wouldn't be surprised if he became Prime Minister! Then she asked Mum if she thought I'd pass my SATS!!! What a cheek!

I'd been going to spend this week treasure hunting with Piper. She found a metal detector in her grandad's shed, and we had stacks of plans.

Now Thomas was coming to stay, Mum would organise all sorts of rubbish stuff.

Things like *board games*, and *blow football*, and **craft**.

I wasn't going to win the 'What I did in my holidays' essay competition by writing about something I made from an egg box, was I?

GRANDMA DANGEROUS
AND THE EGG OF GLORY
Coming soon!

Acknowledgements

Thank you SO MUCH to:

Kate Shaw – Totally Top Agent.
Anna Solemani – Loveliest Editor, ever.
The whole of the amazing team at **Orchard** for bringing Grandma Dangerous to life.
Nathan Reed, for the beautiful pictures.
Everyone from the **Bath Spa MA in Writing for Young People.**
Ruth, for her thorough and most excellent opinions.
My family, for always being there.
Ali, Lorraine, Rob, Jude, Neil, Meryl and Claire, for their never-ending kindness and support. I couldn't have done it without you.

And finally
Isobel, Eva, Hattie and **Daisy**, for all the fun.

Kita Mitchell wrote and illustrated her first work, *Cindersmella*, at the age of six. It was cruelly and swiftly rejected by publishers. The sequels, *Repunsmell* and *Mouldilocks*, were equally badly received.

Disheartened, she turned her attention to making stuff, and, luckily, they did degrees in that. After getting one, she built sets for TV shows – but the feeling she should write funny books for children never went away.

Eventually, she decided to have another go. This time, things turned out a little better. Now, she can tell people she is a proper author, which is great.

Kita currently lives in Oxfordshire with four daughters and a hamster.

@kitamitchell
www.kitamitchell.com

Nathan Reed has been a professional illustrator since graduating from Falmouth College of Arts in 2000. Recent books include *How to Write Your Best Story Ever* and the *Marsh Road Mystery Series*. His latest picture book, written by Angela McAllister, is *Samson the Mighty Flea*. He was also shortlisted for the Serco Prize for Illustration in 2014.